Chapter 1

Knock, knock, knock.

"Go away!"

I'd been working late on a case, and hadn't got in until gone three in the morning. Jack had long since gone to work. I'd woken up just long enough to tell him I wouldn't be going in until lunchtime at the earliest. But now some idiot was knocking at the door.

Knock, knock, knock.

Maybe, if I ignored them, they'd go away.

Knock, knock, knock.

This time it was much louder. They obviously weren't going to take the hint.

I felt dreadful, but I somehow managed to crawl out of bed, and make my way downstairs. I was still in my PJ's, and had bare feet.

Knock, knock, knock.

Whatever happened to patience? Somebody was going to get a piece of my mind.

"At last! I thought you were never going to answer the door."

It was Mrs Mopp. I'd forgotten all about her.

"Sorry, Mrs Mopp. You'd better come in."

She looked me up and down, disapprovingly. "I specifically told you to make sure that everyone in the house was dressed when I arrived."

"Yeah, sorry. I—err—I was working late last night."

"We all have our cross to bear, dear. For instance, I'm standing here talking to you when I could be cleaning."

"Sorry."

"Where's the man of the house? I hope he's not walking

around half naked too."

"Jack's gone to work. I'll go upstairs and get changed."

"Not before time. I'll make a start down here."

The bed looked so inviting. All I wanted to do was crawl back under the covers, and go to sleep, but there was no chance of that with Mrs Mopp downstairs. Somehow, I managed to summon up the strength to shower and get dressed, but I could still barely keep my eyes open. What I needed was coffee—very strong coffee.

"Where do you think you're going?" Mrs Mopp shouted, as I stepped into the kitchen.

"I was going to make myself a coffee."

"I'm in the middle of cleaning the kitchen, you can't possibly come in here. Go and wait in another room until I've finished."

"But I really need—"

"Other room!"

"Right. Okay."

I considered lying on the sofa, but decided that wasn't such a good idea because I'd probably fall asleep. If I did, Mrs Mopp would no doubt lift up the sofa, and throw me onto the floor. I sat in the armchair instead. Ten minutes later, she came in.

"You can use the kitchen now. I'll have a cup of tea."

"Huh? You want *me* to make *you* a cup of tea?"

"Yes, please. And I'll have two custard creams."

"Right. How do you like your tea?"

"No milk, no sugar, and very strong."

I left Mrs Mopp busy in the living room while I made her a cup of tea, and myself the strongest cup of coffee known to man. When I checked the Tupperware box, there were only two custard creams left. Two! That meant none for me. Great! I put them onto a small plate, and took her tea and biscuits through to the living room.

"Don't spill the tea. Put it down there on the table."

I did as I was told, and was just about to sit down.

"You can't be in here while I'm working. You'll have to have your coffee in the kitchen, and don't spill it."

The coffee slowly but surely seemed to wake me up. I spent the next couple of hours dodging Mrs Mopp.

"Ms Gooder!" she called from upstairs. What was wrong now? I was beginning to think I'd rather do the cleaning myself.

"Yes?" I said when I got to the top of the stairs.

"I hope you don't expect me to clean in *there*." She pointed to the spare bedroom. "I can't even get through the door."

"No, of course not. That's—err—that's just full of old furniture."

"Most of it looks like junk."

"It belongs to Jack."

"Really? Does he have no taste?"

After she'd finished, Mrs Mopp took her cleaning materials and equipment back to her car. When she came back into the house, she seemed to be waiting for something.

"Was there something else, Mrs Mopp?"

"The payment?"

"Oh yes, the payment. How much did we say?"

"It's sixty pounds plus materials. We'll call it seventy."

"Right. Err—I'd actually forgotten you were coming today. I don't have any cash on me."

"That isn't a problem." She pulled out a handheld card machine from the pocket of her apron.

"I take all the usual cards."

"Oh? Right. Okay." I found my purse, took out my credit card, and made the payment.

"I'll be back in a fortnight's time at eight-thirty on the dot. Please, no PJ's next time."

"No PJ's. Got it."

***

Mrs Rollo must have been watching through her front window because as soon as I stepped out of the house, she hurried out of her front door.

"Jill! I'm glad I caught you. I baked some scones yesterday, and I thought you and Jack might like some."

"That's—err—very kind of you."

"I'll just go and get them."

Maybe she was better at scones than she was at Victoria sponge cakes?

She wasn't.

"There you go. They're cherry. Is that all right?"

"Yeah, cherry's fine. Thanks, Mrs Rollo. You did say two, didn't you?"

"Yes. One for you, and one for Jack."

"Right, okay. Thank you. I'll take this—err—I mean these inside. Jack and I can have it—err—them tonight."

"Bye then, Jill. Have a good day at work."

I took the solid block of whatever it was into the house. It was impossible to tell where one scone ended, and the other began.

I was just about to climb into the car when I heard an engine. Coming up the pavement, on the opposite side of the road, was what appeared to be a small train, pulling two wooden carriages. As it got closer, I could see the driver. He was wearing a cap, and holding a flag, which he waved at me.

"Morning, Jill."

"Oh? Morning, Mr Hosey."

He brought the train to a halt right across the road from where I was standing.

"Do you like her? I made her myself. I call her Bessie."

"So I see." The name was written in large letters on the side.

"It took me almost eighteen months to build her, but it was worth it, wouldn't you say?"

"Yes—err—do you use it at charity events?"

"No. I won't allow children on Bessie, with their dirty hands and feet. I just drive her around the block: up this street, down Rose Avenue, around Lilac Street, and back up Primrose Avenue. I could take you for a ride if you like? It will only take about twenty minutes."

I checked my watch. "Not right now, thanks, Mr Hosey. I'm actually running late for work as it is. I'd better get going."

"Maybe another time." He tooted his horn, and set the train rolling.

***

I'd just parked in Washbridge when my phone rang. It was Kathy.

"Jill, are you at work?"

"Nearly. I've just arrived in town."

"You lazy madam!"

"I was working on a case until gone three this morning. I'd planned to have a lie in, but then our cleaner turned up."

"You have a cleaner?"

"It wasn't my idea; it was Jack's. He said it would give us more time, but I didn't realise what an ogre she was going to be. She's a right bossy-boots. Almost as bad as you. I had to make tea for her, and she took my last two custard creams."

"Oh dear." Kathy laughed.

"It's not funny. Anyway, what do you want? I've got to get to work."

"I thought I'd let you know I've been offered that job as a presenter at Wool TV."

"Really? Congratulations. You must be thrilled."

"I might not be able to take it."

"Why not?"

"I'd assumed it would be a full-time position, but it's only one day a week and the money isn't great, so there's no way I can give up my job at Ever."

"But surely you still want to do it?"

"Of course I do. I think I'd be good at it, but I don't see how I'm going to manage it. Your grandmother is never going to agree to give me one day off a week, is she?"

"I suppose not. So what are you going to do?"

"I told them I'd have to think about it. Anyway, I'd better let you go."

"Okay. Speak to you later."

***

It was Mrs V's day in.

"Morning, Jill." She looked down in the dumps.

"Are you okay, Mrs V?"

"Yes. I suppose so."

"You don't sound it. What's the matter?"

"I'm not complaining because I know it's my own fault, but I'm beginning to regret going part-time."

"Why?"

"I thought I'd enjoy the rest, but I'm just bored. If Armi was off too, then it wouldn't be so bad; we could do things together. But he's working full-time. I know there's nothing to be done about it. I can't expect you to get rid of Jules; it's not her fault."

"I might have an idea which could help."

"Really? What's that?"

"I was talking to Kathy just now. She's been offered the presenter's job at Wool TV, but it's only one day a week, and not enough money to give up her current job. Maybe you could talk Grandma into letting you cover for Kathy while she works at Wool TV. That way, you get something to occupy your time, and Kathy gets to do her presenting job."

"That would be great." Mrs V's face lit up. "I know I said I'd never work at Ever again, and I certainly wouldn't want to work for your grandmother full-time, but one day a week might be okay. And if it helps Kathy too?"

"Kathy would be thrilled. Why don't you talk to them to see if you can sort something out between the three of you?"

"I will. Is it okay if I go down there now?"

"Of course. Off you go."

"Cuckoo!"

I almost jumped out of my skin. I hadn't noticed the small clock on the wall behind Mrs V.

"You have a clock, Mrs V?"

"Yes. Armi got it for me. They had a two for one offer at the Cuckoo Clock Appreciation Society. Do you like it?"

"Err—yeah, it's—err—very nice. I'm not sure if I've ever seen a cuckoo clock in an office before."

"That's why I thought it would be such a good idea. And, you'll be pleased to know I've put one in your office as well."

"Great! Tell Armi thank you for me, would you?"

"Of course."

A cuckoo clock? What sort of impression would that give to a prospective client if halfway through a serious conversation, a bird popped its head out, and started cuckooing? But I could hardly take it down; Mrs V would be mortally offended.

When I walked into my office, I found Winky sitting on the sofa; he was staring at the cuckoo clock which Mrs V had put on the wall above the sofa.

"Winky?"

"Don't talk to me now, I'm busy."

"Doing what?"

"There's a bird in that box up there. The next time it sticks its head out, I'm going to have it."

"You do realise that's a clock, don't you?"

"I don't care what it is. There's a bird inside it, and when it comes out again, it's dead meat!"

"But it's not actually a real bird."

"Of course it's a real bird. It keeps coming out and

tweeting at me."

"Does it make a sound a bit like this, 'Cuckoo, cuckoo'?"

"That's it! That's exactly how it sounds."

Oh boy! Winky was something of an enigma. The cat was the mastermind behind any number of money-making schemes, and yet here he was, apparently convinced that the bird inside the cuckoo clock was real.

Wow! Just wow!

Only then, did I notice that the floor close to my desk was covered in cogs, nuts, bolts, brackets, spanners, screwdrivers, and all manner of things mechanical.

"What exactly have you been doing here, Winky? Why is all this stuff all over my office floor?"

"I'm building something. Can't you see?"

"Building what?"

"If I told you, you'd only mock."

"I would never mock you, Winky."

"You mock everyone. That's what you do."

"I promise I won't mock. What are you building?"

"It's a time machine."

"A time machine?" I burst out laughing. "Of course it is."

"What did I just say? I said you'd mock."

"I'm not mocking; I'm just laughing. There's no such thing as a time machine."

"Don't be so certain. Look, you're a witch, right?"

"Yeah?"

"And you routinely travel backwards and forwards to another land where supernatural creatures live?"

"Yeah."

"So, it's okay to believe in all of that stuff, but a bit of time travel? That's too weird?"
"It's not weird; it's impossible."
"We'll see, won't we?"
"Okay, if it amuses you. You carry on playing with your Meccano."
"This is not Meccano. I'll have you know, I am a serious engineer."
"Of course you are."
"I take it that you don't believe in time travel?"
"Of course I don't. It's nonsense."
"So you'd be willing to have a little wager?"
"Of course I would." This was easy money. "How much do you want to bet?"
"A hundred pounds?"
"Make it two hundred." I shouldn't take advantage of the poor fool, but it would do him good if I taught him a lesson.
"Two hundred pounds it is," he agreed.
Easy money. Snigger. "Whatever it is you're building, you can't have this clutter all over the office floor. You'll have to work in that corner. And get a screen so you don't freak out my clients."
"What clients?" He laughed.

Chapter 2

The previous day, I'd had a phone call from a Maisy Topp. She'd asked if she could come to see me. I'd tried to find out what it was all about, but she'd been reluctant to discuss it over the phone. Never one to turn a prospective client away, I'd agreed that she could come in today.

Maisy was in her fifties, and sported a cute red hat which sat precariously on top of her greying hair.

"Maisy, come in, do take a seat. Can I get you a drink? Tea? Coffee?"

"No, I'm fine thanks. I'm not fond of hot drinks."

"What about a glass of water?"

"No, thank you."

"Did you find my office okay?"

"Yes. I saw your sign."

Thankfully, I'd managed to sort out the signage problem. I'd stood Sid Song in front of the building, and asked him what he thought he was playing at. He'd been confused until I'd pointed out that the sign had appeared to read:

Jill Gooder
Private Investigator
I-Sweat

Only then had he realised why I was so annoyed. After a little 'friendly' persuasion he'd admitted it was his fault, and had provided me with a replacement sign, in a different font and colour, free of charge. The two signs were now far enough apart to avoid any embarrassment or confusion.

"How can I help you today, Maisy?"

"My dog, Toto, has gone missing."

I hadn't been expecting that. I got quite a few missing person cases, but I'd never been approached about a missing dog before.

"I see. This dog of yours. Is it a show dog? Has he won prizes?"

"No, nothing like that. He's just a regular poodle."

"Have you been in touch with the local dog pound to see if he's been handed in?"

"Yes. I've contacted all the usual places. But no one's seen him."

"Was he wearing a name tag?"

"Of course. He wears his collar all the time. It's quite distinctive. It has diamonds on it."

"Real diamonds?"

"Yes."

"How many?"

"Four."

"It must be worth quite a bit?"

"I suppose so. I've never really thought about it. Nothing is too good for Toto."

While it was entirely possible that someone might want to steal a poodle, they were much more likely to have been after the diamond studded collar. My immediate concern was that whoever had taken the dog, may have already discarded poor old Toto. Of course, I wasn't about to say that to Maisy. She already looked rather fragile.

"Where and how did this happen?"

"I'd gone to pick up my magazine from the newsagent.

I was parked in the car park across the road from the shop. I'm only ever in there for a few minutes, so I often leave Toto in the back of the car. Of course, I always keep the window down a little so he doesn't get overheated, and I always park in the shade."

"And when you got back to the car?"

"Toto had gone. I looked everywhere. I walked up and down the street, and asked everyone I came across. But no one had seen him."

"You didn't happen to notice if there were any CCTV cameras in the car park or on the street, did you?"

"There aren't. It's one of the first things I thought about. None at all, I'm afraid."

"Have you been to the police about this?"

"Yes, but they more or less told me they were too busy to do anything about a missing dog."

"Did you mention the diamond-studded collar?"

"Yes, but that didn't seem to make a lot of difference."

"Do you have a photograph of Toto?"

"Lots of them." She opened her handbag, and took out four or five photos which she put on the desk in front of me. "That's him. He's a handsome boy, isn't he?"

Seen one dog, seen them all. "Yes. Very handsome."

"Do you think you'll be able to help?"

"I don't know—I have to be honest with you, Maisy. I've never had a missing dog case before."

"I just need some hope to cling onto. Money is no object."

Music to my ears. "Of course. Why don't I give it a shot for a few days, and see what I can come up with?"

"That would be great." She checked her watch. "Sorry, I have to go. I'm on the town council, and I have a meeting in fifteen minutes. You've got my phone number, haven't you?"

"Yes, you gave it to me yesterday when you called."

"Good. Please let me know straight away if you find anything. I'm desperate to get Toto back."

"Sure. I'll do my best."

Mrs V came through to my office. I could tell by her face that she had good news.

"Did you see Grandma?"

"Yes, and Kathy. The three of us had a good chat. Surprisingly, your grandmother seemed quite open to the idea. She said Kathy would have to liaise with me, so I know which day I need to cover for her. I explained that I still work here some days, but your grandmother said not to worry about that because obviously her shop was more important."

"She did, did she? That's nice to know."

"Is it all right, Jill? For me to do this?"

"Yes, it'll be fine. By the way, how are the preparations going for the dinner and dance with Armi?"

"Okay. I haven't danced in a while so I'm a bit rusty, but Armi and I have been meeting up in the evenings at the local social club to get some practice. I'm hopeful, by the day of the dance, we'll be on top form."

Just then, someone walked into the outer office.

"Are you expecting anyone, Jill?"

"No. I've no more appointments."

"I'll go and see who it is." Mrs V went to check.

"It's a young woman. She says she's a neighbour of yours. Her name's Jen."

"Oh? Please show her in."

When Jen came through, she looked worried.

"Hi, Jen. I wasn't expecting to see you."

"It was a spur-of-the-moment decision. I hadn't planned on doing this, and I'm still not sure I should be here."

"Would you like a cup of tea?"

"That would be nice."

"Mrs V, could you make some tea for us, please?"

"Milk and sugar?" she asked Jen.

"Milk no sugar, please."

"I'll have my usual sugar quotient please, Mrs V."

She scowled at me.

"So, what exactly is it that brings you here today, Jen?"

"Do you remember the other night when I came over to your place? When I said I couldn't shake the feeling there was something that Blake wasn't telling me? Almost as though there's a part of his life that I know nothing about?"

"Yeah?" I didn't like the way this was heading.

"I've had the same nagging worry now for some time, and it isn't going away. If we're ever going to have children, I need to get rid of this silly suspicion."

"When you say suspicion, what is it exactly you think he might have done?"

"That's just it. I don't know. I feel like there's something he's holding back from me. I sometimes wonder if there's someone else."

"Surely not. I've seen you and Blake together. You make a lovely couple; he obviously dotes on you."

"I know, and I feel terrible even suggesting it, but the feeling isn't going to go away unless I can be absolutely sure. That's why I'm here today. You won't tell him, will you?"

"No, of course not. But what exactly is it you want me to do?"

"Find out if there is something going on that I should know about. I need someone to put my mind at rest. Will you do it, Jill?"

"It would put me in a very awkward position. Blake's a friend too."

"I know. But I'd rather you did it than some stranger."

"Are you absolutely sure about this?"

"Positive."

"Okay then."

Jen and I talked for another fifteen minutes while we drank our tea. During that time, I was trying to work out what on earth I was going to do about this situation. I already knew what Blake was keeping from her because I was doing exactly the same thing with Jack. But I could hardly tell her that her husband was a wizard. Should I tell Blake? He was a friend too, and a fellow sup. Maybe, if I made him aware of Jen's concerns, he could do something to alleviate them.

Oh dear. What a mess.

***

I needed a break, so I magicked myself over to Cuppy C. To my surprise, working behind the counter, was Laura, one of the two witches who were now living in the rooms upstairs.

"Laura? What are you doing behind there?"

"I work here now. Amber and Pearl knew that I was looking for a job back in Candlefield because I'd had enough of working in the human world. They offered me a position here. It's not as many hours as I was working in Washbridge, and the money's not as good, but I'm just happy to be back among sups. Is there something I can get you?"

"I'd like one of your blueberry muffins, please. And a caramel latte."

As she passed me the muffin, my hand grazed hers. It was icy cold again—just as it had been when I shook hands with her the first time we'd met. It was warm in Cuppy C, so why on earth was she so cold?

She was about to put the items through the till.

"You know I get staff discount, don't you?"

"Yes, Amber and Pearl told me."

Just then, the twins came through from the cake shop.

"I hope you didn't give her that for free," Amber said.

Laura shook her head. "I've only given her the staff discount."

"Good." Amber grinned.

The twins followed me to the window table.

"Business must be good if you've set on another member of staff?"

"One of our other assistants left. Laura had mentioned she was looking for a job back in Candlefield, so we thought why not? She's doing very well. She's picked things up really quickly."

"Quicker than me, you mean?"

"Jill. Everybody's quicker than you."

"Thanks. You know how to make a girl feel good."

"I'm sure you're a really good private investigator, but you're rubbish behind that counter."

"You're right, I know."

"Hey, Jill." Pearl was obviously bursting to tell me

something. “Do you want to hear our big plans?”

“What is it this time? Have you decided to invest in a snake oil factory?”

“Nothing like that. We’ve decided it’s time that we expanded the Cuppy C empire.”

“You mean open another shop in Candlefield?”

“Not in Candlefield,” Amber said. “We’re going to open a shop in—”

“Washbridge!” Pearl jumped in.

“Washbridge?” Oh no! “Whereabouts?”

“You know that shop across the road from Ever A Wool Moment?”

“You mean where Miles Best had his wool shop?”

“That’s the one.”

“Directly across the road from Grandma’s knitting shop and tea room?”

“Yep,” Pearl said.

“Are you two absolutely insane?”

The twins had gone off to sulk because I didn’t share their enthusiasm for the expansion plans. Not long after, Hilary from Love Spell walked into the shop.

“Hi, Jill. Long time, no see.”

“I’m glad I bumped into you. Could I have a word?”

“Sure, let me just get a drink. Can I get you anything? A top-up or another muffin?”

“No, I’m fine, thanks.”

See? I do have willpower.

“What can I do for you, Jill?” Hilary joined me at the table.

“I have a bit of a dilemma, and I really don’t know what to do about it. I’d value your advice.”

"What's that?"

"I recently moved into a new house in Smallwash."

"Oh, yes, I know it. It's just over the toll bridge, isn't it?"

"Yeah, that's it. Anyway, there's a young couple living directly across the road from me. He's a wizard; she's a human."

"So pretty much the reverse of you and Jack, then."

"That's right."

"What's the problem?"

"The young woman, Jen, came to see me, earlier today. She's concerned because she feels her husband, Blake, is keeping something from her. She feels like there's a part of his life that she doesn't know anything about."

"Yeah, well, she's right, isn't she?"

"Of course she's right. It's the same with me and Jack, but fortunately Jack hasn't cottoned on yet. At least, I hope he hasn't. Jen actually thinks that Blake might be having an affair."

"That's not good."

"She's asked if I'd investigate to see what I can find out."

"Did you say you would?"

"I didn't really have any choice."

"What are you going to tell her?"

"I don't know. Do you think I should talk to Blake? Should I tell him that Jen's been to see me?"

"That's a difficult one. If you do, you're betraying the trust of Jen, but then again if you don't, you're being unfair to Blake. There's no good answer, but my gut feeling is that you should tell him. You're both sups, so he'll understand, and maybe there's something he can do to alleviate Jen's worries."

"I think you're right. I'm going to have to talk to him."

I'd finished my drink and muffin, and was just on my way out when Alan and William walked in.

"Ah, Jill, I'm glad I caught you," William said.

"What can I do for you?"

"Is it right what I've heard? Are you an elder now?"

"Do I look like an elder?"

"You know what I mean. Are you on the board of the Combined Sup Council?"

"I haven't been to a meeting yet, but yes, I'm hoping I'll be able to make a contribution."

"Good. It's time they had some new blood on there. There's something that we'd like you to put forward."

"What's that?"

"Can you get them to stop blocking the introduction of the internet in Candlefield?"

"I didn't realise it was the Combined Sup Council who have been blocking it."

"In theory, there's nothing to stop us having the internet here, but every time it's proposed, they come out against it. Even though they don't have any real power, nobody wants to go against their wishes. At this rate, it's never going to happen. It's doing our heads in—we have to go to Washbridge just to get online—it's crazy. Will you see what you can do?"

"I can't promise anything. I need to check out the lay of the land first. But yeah, if the opportunity presents itself, then I'll certainly push for it. I think it would be a great idea."

"Thanks, Jill. We knew you'd understand."

Chapter 3

"But, Jack, I've got stomach ache and I feel nauseous."

"No, you don't, Jill. You're lying."

"How can you say that?"

"Easily. This is all because you don't want to go."

"Of course I do."

"No you don't. You've done nothing but moan about it ever since Kathy booked the tickets."

"But who in their right mind would want to see 'Ultimate Factor Live'?"

"Me, for one. And Kathy and Peter. We promised we'd go, and that's what we're going to do. You'd better hurry up and get ready because they're coming to pick us up in thirty-five minutes."

"But—"

"Go and get changed, Jill."

"You really hate me, don't you?"

I stormed upstairs. I'd been dreading this night ever since Kathy had told me she had the tickets. Ultimate Factor Live? Those TV talent shows were terrible; all of the acts were awful. To make matters worse, the top of the bill was none other than my old friends, The Coven. They'd once offered me a place in their dance troupe. All I'd had to do was learn a bit of a dance routine, and say the 'The.' If I'd said 'yes,' I'd have been famous by now, and would have made a small fortune. Kathy, Peter and Jack would have been going to see me tonight. Instead, I was having to pay good money to watch The Coven, and the other no-hopers.

I got changed slowly, hoping for some divine intervention, but half an hour later Jack shouted.

"Peter and Kathy are here. Are you ready?"

"Nearly. I still don't feel very well, though."

"Get your backside down here, quick."

Some people have no compassion.

Peter drove, which left Kathy free to give Jack an ear-bashing all the way there.

"It's going to be great," she said. "I can't wait to see The Coven."

"Yeah, me too." Jack nodded.

I was beginning to have serious doubts about the man.

"Did you know that Jill had a chance to be in The Coven?" Kathy and her big mouth.

"Don't be ridiculous." He laughed.

"It's true," Kathy insisted. "Tell him, Jill."

I shrugged.

"Ignore her. She's being a misery guts as always," Kathy said. "If she won't tell you, I will. The Coven offered Jill the chance to be the 'The', but she turned it down."

Jack turned to me. "Is that right?"

I shrugged again.

"You turned down the chance to be in The Coven?"

"Yes, I turned them down. So what?"

"You would have been rich and famous. We could have had a great big house somewhere out in the countryside."

"Yeah, well, I don't care."

"She does really," Kathy said. "She's still kicking herself. Anyway, I sent them an email."

"Sent who an email?" I didn't like the sound of that.

"The Coven, or at least their management."

"What do you mean you sent them an email?"

"I told them you'd be coming tonight."

"Please tell me you didn't."

"I did, why not?"

Great!

"I shouldn't worry about it," Peter said. "They must get tons of emails; they won't take any notice of it."

"They'd better not. If you embarrass me, Kathy, I'm going to kill you." It was time to bring up Kathy's favourite subject. "When's Megan Lovemore coming around, Peter?"

"Yes, Pete." Kathy spat the words. "When *is* Megan coming around?"

"Tomorrow, actually," Peter said. "Thanks for stirring it, Jill."

"I don't know what you mean," I said, all butter-wouldn't-melt like. "She only wants some advice on her new business plan, doesn't she?"

"She'd better not think she's going to stay for long." Kathy was still glaring at Peter.

"There's a lot of stuff I have to go over with her," he said.

"Yeah, well you'd better talk fast. I'm going to be sitting in there with you, stopwatch in hand."

"There's no need for that, Kathy. Surely you trust me."

"I trust *you*, Pete, I just don't trust *her*."

Ultimate Factor Live was every bit as good as I'd expected it to be. The first act was a man with a performing donkey. And if I tell you that was the highlight of the show, it will perhaps give you a flavour of what I had to put up with. But it seemed I was in a minority of one because everyone else in the Washbridge Arena seemed to love it. They laughed, they clapped, and they shouted for more. I shouted, 'Get off,' but nobody could hear me. The whole thing was supposed to last for three hours, but I felt like I'd already been there for the best part of a month, and the top of the bill was yet to come on stage.

"It's The Coven next," Kathy said.

"Yeah, yeah. So what?"

The three women, led by Brenda, walked onto the stage. If I wasn't mistaken, they'd invested in slightly more upmarket leotards. They went straight into their first number. Even I had to admit they'd improved since I'd last seen them. Their dance routines were a lot slicker; perhaps they'd invested in a choreographer. Don't get me wrong, it was still absolutely terrible. It just wasn't *as* terrible as before. When it came to their finale, the crowd was absolutely buzzing with anticipation. The three women got down on one knee, and then jumped up one by one.

"We. Are. The Coven."

The crowd shouted, screamed, and waved their hands about. They couldn't get enough of them.

"That could have been you." Kathy nudged me.

"Shut up."

When the applause finally died down, Brenda stepped up to the mic.

"Thank you. Thank you. You're all so kind. We've come such a long way in such a short period of time, and we owe it all to you. You're the ones who voted us through week after week. Never in our wildest dreams did we imagine we'd be here tonight. But before we go, we want to mention someone very special who's in the arena tonight."

Kathy looked at me. Peter looked at me. Jack looked at me. I prayed that the floor would open up and swallow me.

"We want to give a big shout out to Jill Gooder. Please, put the spotlight on her."

Oh, no! The next minute I was blinded by the beam.

"Most of you won't know Jill," Brenda continued. "But we owe her more than you can ever know. Jill, we just wanted to say a big thank you for TDO."

With that, the spotlight went off, and The Coven left the stage. Everyone was staring at me. I just wanted to get out of there, and quickly.

"Come on, let's go." I led the way out.

When we eventually made it back to the car, Kathy began with the interrogation. "What was that all about? What's TDO?"

"Err—TDO? Oh yeah, they asked me for some advice—about their dance routine, and I suggested Total Dance Optimisation."

"Total what?"

"You wouldn't understand, Kathy. It's very complex."

***

Jack was a good cook. At least, he was a lot better than me. But the man simply could not make toast. It was either white or burnt to a crisp. This morning, it was the latter—black.

"Do you think maybe you overdid the toast, today?"

"I like my toast crispy."

"This isn't crispy. It's practically charcoal."

"You know where the toaster is if you think you can do

any better."

"I don't have time."

"You'd better eat it then." He joined me at the breakfast bar. "I still can't believe you never mentioned The Coven to me."

"There was nothing to tell."

"What do you mean nothing? You were offered the chance to join the UK's premier dance troupe."

"They weren't the UK's premier dance troupe when they approached me. They were a little known dance troupe taking part in talent contests in and around Washbridge."

"Even so, you missed a golden opportunity."

"I'd rather you didn't keep reminding me."

"Is there anything else you haven't told me?"

"What do you mean?"

"Any little secrets in your life which you're keeping from me?"

Little did he know that there was a whopper of a secret that I could never share with him.

"No. You know everything there is to know about me. I'm an open book."

Jack left for work, and I followed a few minutes later. As I stepped out of the door, someone called to me. It was Megan.

"Jill, have you got a minute?"

"I'm on my way to work."

"It'll only take a second."

"Okay." I walked over to the fence.

She was dressed in vest and shorts, which seemed to be her outfit of choice in and around the house. As always, she looked stunning.

"I'm going to see Peter today," she said.

"Jack and I were out with him and Kathy last night."

"I'm really grateful to you for arranging it."

"No problem."

"I feel like I'm taking up a lot of Peter's time, and I'd like to do something by way of a thank you. Is there anything I could get for him? As a token of appreciation?"

"If I were you, I'd buy a nice bunch of flowers for Kathy. She'd like that, and I think Peter would appreciate the gesture."

"That's a great idea, thanks."

I was just about to get in the car when I noticed Jen driving up the road. She spotted me, and waved as she drove past.

Blake's car was still on the driveway. It was an ideal opportunity to have a quick word with him, so I walked over and knocked on the door.

"Jill?" He seemed surprised to see me. "Is everything okay?"

"Yeah—no—I think so."

"Do you want to come in?"

"No, thanks. I don't have time. I'm on my way to work. Look, I'm not sure whether I should tell you this or not." I hesitated.

"You have to, now that you've started."

"You mustn't mention it to Jen."

"Mention *what* to her?"

"That I'm telling you this. She dropped by my office yesterday. She's concerned about you."

"Why would she be concerned about me?"

"She came over to my place the other night while you were away on business. She said she thought you might be hiding something. Maybe even seeing someone else behind her back. Then yesterday, she popped into my office, and asked me to follow you to see if anything was going on."

"Wow! She must really be worried. But what can I do? If I tell her I'm a wizard, she'll think I'm crazy. And if I proved it to her by doing magic, I'd leave myself open to being taken back to Candlefield by the Rogue Retrievers."

"I understand your dilemma, believe me. But you need to put Jen's mind at rest somehow. She's obviously got a bee in her bonnet."

"You have to help me, Jill."

"What can I do?"

"It's lucky she came to you. She could have gone to another P.I. Why don't you pretend to follow me for a few days, and then report back to her? Confirm that I'm not doing anything behind her back, and that I'm not seeing anyone."

"I don't know. It doesn't feel right."

"There's no other way to put her mind at rest. Please, Jill, will you do it?"

"Okay, if you're sure."

"I'm sure."

***

Jules was behind the desk today.

"Jill, you have to do something about that stupid thing." She gestured to the cuckoo clock.

"What's wrong with it?"

"It's driving me potty. Every hour, on the hour, it pops its little head out, and starts making that stupid cuckoo noise."

"That's what cuckoo clocks do, Jules."

"I know, but who has a cuckoo clock in their office? How am I meant to focus on my knitting with that thing cuckooing all the time?"

"There isn't much I can do about it. It belongs to Mrs V; it was a present from Armi. I can hardly tell her to take it down, can I?"

"Can't you just hit it with something?"

"No, I can't hit it with something. How would I explain that away? 'Oh, sorry Mrs V. I accidentally hit your cuckoo clock with something'."

"I suppose you're right. I'll have to bring my iPod to work, and listen to music."

"Just make sure you can still hear the phone ring."

"By the way, Jill, did you find out if those two guys who work for your brother-in-law have girlfriends?"

"Not yet, but I will. I promise."

"Thanks, Jill."

When I walked into my office, there was what looked like the remains of the cuckoo on the floor. I couldn't see Winky, but I could hear him. He was working behind the screen.

"Winky, get out here now!"

He walked slowly around the screen. "What? Can't you see I'm busy? I was in the middle of fitting a transponder."

"I don't care about your transponder. What's this?" I pointed to the remains of the cuckoo.

"It's that stupid mechanical bird."

"The one you thought was real?"

"I did *not* think it was real."

"Yes you did. You were trying to catch it."

"I was only winding you up. You're so gullible. Anyway, the stupid thing was driving me insane with its cuckooing, so I took it out."

"What will Mrs V say?"

"Who cares what the old bag lady says? She's not the one who has to listen to it."

He went back behind the screen, and carried on working. If I was being perfectly honest, I was pleased he'd taken out the clock. I found it hard to focus at the best of times, but with that thing cuckooing every hour, it was nigh on impossible. But what was I going to tell Mrs V? Maybe if I hid what was left of the bird, she wouldn't notice. Provided, that is, she didn't come into my office on the hour.

Chapter 4

I hadn't been at my desk for more than fifteen minutes when I felt a chill in the air. My first thought was that my father might be paying me another visit, but it turned out to be my mother this time.

"Hi, Mum. How's things?"

"Is it true what I've heard?" She snapped.

"I don't know. What have you heard?"

"I heard a rumour that your father has attached himself to you."

"Yeah, he did. He came to see me the other day."

"And you allowed him to?"

"I thought it would give me a chance to get to know him."

"He didn't want to know you when you were born, or when you were growing up. It's a bit late to want to get to know you now he's dead, isn't it?"

"I know he left you in the lurch, but he did try to save my life when I had the showdown with TDO."

"And I'm very grateful that he did. Although, you would make a good ghost."

"Don't say that. It gives me the creeps."

"There's nothing that man could do that would ever compensate for all the years when he was out of your life. I'd suggest you tell him to get lost."

"I'm not going to do that. I want to at least give him a chance."

"Well, if that's how you feel—" And with that, she disappeared.

Oh, dear. It never occurred to me that getting to know my father might upset my mother. Even so, I was going to give him the benefit of the doubt. My mother would just have to get used to the idea.

I couldn't bear the thought of Jules making a drink. The spillage was more trouble than it was worth.

"I'm just nipping to Coffee Triangle, Jules. And while I'm passing, I'll call in at Ever A Wool Moment to see Kathy, and Mrs V if she's there."

"Mrs V? Why would she be there?"

"She's decided she doesn't like the shorter working week, and is looking for something to fill her time. I suggested she might cover for Kathy at Ever. She's been offered a job presenting on Wool TV."

"I didn't know there was such a thing as Wool TV. Mrs V never mentioned it."

"It's probably not your thing. It's mainly for older people."

"I'd like to see it. I'm really into knitting now. I bet it's really exciting."

"I'm not sure I'd call it exciting. Instructional, maybe. You might get some tips. Anyway, as I was saying, Kathy's been offered a job there. It's only one day a week, and she didn't think she'd be able to get time off from Ever. That's why I suggested that Mrs V could cover for her."

"That's a great idea."

"I'd better get going. I'll see you later."

When I arrived at Ever, Mrs V was behind the counter with Kathy, who appeared to be showing her the ropes.

"Hello, you two. How's it going?"

"Hi, Jill," Mrs V beamed. "I think I'm going to enjoy working here one day a week."

"Thanks for suggesting this, Jill," Kathy said. "It's a brilliant idea. It means I can take the Wool TV job. And your grandmother seems okay with it."

"That's great. I'm glad it worked out for you both. By the way, Kathy, I saw Megan this morning."

Kathy's face fell. "What did she want?"

"She said she was looking forward to going over to your place this afternoon to see Peter."

"Oh crumbs, I'd forgotten about that. I'd better make sure I'm back in time. I'm not leaving her alone with Pete. I wouldn't trust her as far as I could throw her."

"I'm going to Coffee Triangle. Do you want to join me?"

"I can't. I want to run through a few more things with Mrs V, and I have to make sure I get away on the dot, so I'll be back home before Ms Megan arrives. I'll catch you later."

It was maracas day in Coffee Triangle. There were a few people shaking their maracas at the other end of the shop, but I deliberately found a quiet corner seat. Someone had left a copy of The Bugle on the table, so I took a quick flick through it. It was full of the usual, low quality, gutter journalism, but one thing did catch my eye. It wasn't an article, but a large advert for a missing dog. Someone was offering a two-hundred pounds reward for the safe return of a Westie called Hector. Could this have any connection to Toto's disappearance? Were there dog thieves in the city? I made a note of the phone number listed in the ad.

I was on the point of leaving Coffee Triangle when I heard someone call my name. It was Mad; she was with her mother, Delilah. Oh boy. Mad looked thoroughly fed up. When Delilah went to the counter to order drinks, Mad came over to join me.

"Rescue me, Jill, please."

"What's going on?"

"You'll never believe it. My mother's getting married."

I glanced across at Delilah.

"Not to Nails, surely?"

"Oh yeah. To Nails."

"So, Nails is going to be your dad?" I laughed.

"Step Dad," she insisted. "What did I do to deserve this?"

"What are you two up to, anyway?"

"She's been dragging me around town to look for her wedding dress. As if I'm in any position to give her advice." Mad glanced over, just to make sure her mother couldn't hear us. "Besides which, you know what Mum's like. You've seen the way she dresses."

"But surely she'll dress differently for her own wedding?"

"It makes no difference to Mum. We've spent the best part of three hours looking at some of the skankiest dresses you've ever seen in your life."

Delilah looked around to see where Mad was. She spotted us and came over.

"Hello there, Jill. I didn't realise you were here. I would have got you a drink. Would you like something?"

"No, I'm okay, thanks, Mrs Lane."

"Don't call me Mrs Lane. I've told you, it's Deli."

"Right, okay, Deli. I was just about to leave—"

"Don't go yet! Has Madeline told you my exciting news?" She hustled Mad along the bench seat, so she could sit opposite me.

"That you're getting married? Yeah. Congratulations." Or commiserations, one of the two.

"It came totally out of the blue," she said. "I was eating fish and chips, and Nails was treating his corns. Then suddenly he said, 'Wanna get married?' It was so romantic. It fair took my breath away!"

"I can see how it would."

"I said yes, obviously. A girl can't turn down a catch like Nails. Madeline tells me you've got yourself a young man, at last."

"Yeah, I'm living with Jack now out in Smallwash."

"Good for you. Now you need to start pumping out some young-uns."

Pumping out?

"We're not ready for children yet, Deli. Maybe in a few years' time."

"It's never too early to start. We've been looking at dresses all morning. We've seen some beauties, haven't we, Madeline?"

Mad rolled her eyes, but said nothing.

"I think the nicest was that last one we looked at." Deli slurped her coffee. "The one in Top Dress. You know, that red one?"

Mad shook her head. "You can't possibly mean the one that just about covered your bum?"

"It wasn't that short!"

"And so low you could almost see your navel."

"Take no notice of her, Jill. She's always exaggerating."

"It wasn't suitable for a wedding, Mum."

"'Course it was! It was a beautiful dress. I would have bought it there and then if you hadn't made me have second thoughts. I still might. I ought to go back and get it before someone else beats me to it."

"I shouldn't worry on that score, Mum. What about your varicose veins?"

"I'll wear tights. Anyway, Jill, I'm glad I've seen you because we're going to be sending out the wedding invitations soon. You'll have to give me your new address because I want you and your fella—what's his name, again?"

"Jack."

"I want you and Jack to come. You will come, won't you?"

I could see a grin spreading across Mad's face.

"Yeah, of course. Providing we're not already doing something that day."

"Great! Look, I can't stop thinking about that red dress." She gulped down the rest of her coffee. "I'm going to nip back and get it before someone else does. Madeline, you stay here with Jill, and make sure you let me have her new address, so I can send her an invite."

"Okay, Mum."

"Bye then, Jill."

"Bye, Mrs—Deli."

"Thank goodness she's gone," Mad said. "That dress is ten shades of horrible."

"What is she thinking, marrying Nails?"

"I don't know. I only found out myself a few days ago. It's like some sort of nightmare. I keep hoping I'll wake up."

"Has Nails got any better?"

"In what respect?"

"Any respect."

"If anything he's worse. I don't go around to Mum's

any more often than I have to. But every time I do, I spend most of the time dodging his toenails. He's a horrible man. I don't know what Mum sees in him."

"What about you, Mad? Are you seeing anyone at the moment?"

"Actually, I am."

"And you look pretty pleased about it."

"Yeah. This guy is a cut above some of the others I've been out with recently. His name's Henry."

"And what does Henry do?"

"He's a Ghost Hunter too."

"Really? I thought you were the only Ghost Hunter in Washbridge."

"I was until recently. But we've had so many incidents in and around Washbridge that the powers that be in Ghost Town decided it needed a two-man operation to cover the area. So Henry was transferred from somewhere else in the country."

"What does Henry do when he's not ghost hunting? Does he work at the library with you?"

"No. It would be too dangerous to have two Ghost Hunters using the same cover job. Do you know that little arcade, close to Washbridge Library?"

"The one with the really small shops inside?"

"That's the one. There's a stamp collectors' shop in there. Henry's working there."

"Stamp collecting?"

"He isn't into stamps, but it's an ideal cover for a Ghost Hunter. He's bored out of his mind, much like me, but what can you do?"

"You said there's been a lot of ghost activity?"

"There has, and it's going to get worse. Something's

going on, Jill. I don't know what it is, but in all the time I've been in Washbridge, I've never known so much ghost activity."

"Should I be worried?"

"I don't know. If it carries on like this, I'm not sure even two Ghost Hunters will be able to keep it under control. If we don't, and word gets out, there could be mass panic. Hopefully it won't come to that."

Mad's phone rang.

"I have to take this. It's Henry. Hi, sexy. No, I'm having a coffee with Jill. Remember I told you about her? Yeah."

"I've got to go, Mad," I mouthed. "Catch you later."

Mad was obviously smitten with her new guy.

Chapter 5

The next morning, I decided to pay a visit to Aunt Lucy. It was a while since I'd checked on Barry and Hamlet. They were probably beginning to think I'd abandoned them.

I magicked myself over to Candlefield, and was surprised to find Lester at home. He was at the kitchen table, and had a newspaper and notepad in front of him.

"Hello, Jill," he said, barely managing a smile.

"Hi, Lester. I don't see you very often these days."

"You'll probably be seeing a lot more of me, I'm afraid."

"Oh? Why's that?"

"I've lost my job."

"I thought you were really busy?"

"We were. That's why it came as something of a shock. Apparently the company has been losing money for some time, so they've had to let about half of the workforce go. I was one of the unlucky ones."

"I'm really sorry to hear that. Are you looking for something else?"

"Yeah, that's why I've got the newspaper. There isn't much available at the moment, but I guess I'll have to keep trying. I'm too young to retire." He laughed, but it was a hollow laugh.

Just then, Aunt Lucy came into the room.

"Jill, hi! How lovely to see you!"

"Lester's been telling me his bad news."

"Yes. It's very disappointing, but worse things happen. We'll get through it, won't we Lester?"

"Of course we will." He sounded less than convinced.

"Cup of tea?" Aunt Lucy offered.

"That would be lovely, and then I'll take Barry for a walk."

"You'll be lucky." She laughed. "He's dead to the world. Lester and I took him for a long walk this morning. Much longer than usual. When we got back, he was absolutely shattered. He's fast asleep upstairs. I don't think he'll be going on any more walks until much later in the day."

"Oh? Okay. I'll go and say hello to Hamlet while you make the tea."

"You know where he is, don't you?"

He was in one of the spare bedrooms.

"Hello, stranger," Hamlet said.

"Hi, Hamlet."

"Nice of you to find the time to visit." No one did sarcasm quite like a hamster.

"I'm sorry I haven't been to see you for a while."

"For far too long! And I don't remember being consulted about being moved from the shop to here."

"Don't you like it here?"

"As it happens, I do. It's much better than the other place. I have a lot more space than I had in that little cupboard I was in before. Still, it would have been nice to be consulted."

"How's the reading club going?"

"Very well. Some of the members complained because the move meant they had to travel a little further, but I think they've all got used to the idea now. We've covered one or two good books recently. What about you, Jill? Have you done much reading lately?"

"Lately? Not a lot, to be honest." None, to be precise.

"You really should. You need to keep your mind active. As you get older, the brain cells start to disappear."

Cheek!

"I suppose I'd better get back downstairs. Aunt Lucy is making me a cup of tea."

"Before you go, there are a couple of things I wanted to talk to you about."

Oh dear. Usually, when Hamlet wanted to talk to me, it cost me money.

"What's that, Hamlet?"

"Firstly, I've heard that you are now on the board of the Combined Sup Council."

"How on earth did you hear about that?"

"The rodent grapevine is alive and well here in Candlefield. So, is it true?"

"It is, yes. But I haven't actually attended my first meeting yet."

"I have just the issue for you to raise."

"You do? What's that?"

"The internet. We desperately need it here in Candlefield. Although we rodents are fortunate to have RodentNet, it has limitations. I need access to the wider internet."

"It's curious you should mention that because the twins' husbands actually approached me on the very same subject. They want me to bring up the issue with the Council too."

"Will you?"

"I'll need to find my feet first, but I'll definitely bring it up at the first opportunity."

"Good."

"You said there was something else?"

"This is a rather delicate matter. I trust I can rely on you to be discreet."

"Discretion is my middle name."

"I get a little lonely sometimes." He sighed.

"What about the book club?"

"That's all very nice, but what I really need is female company. One on one, if you know what I mean?"

The last thing I wanted was dozens of little hamsters running around the place. Still, it was understandable that Hamlet might be lonely.

"Would you like me to go to the pet shop to buy a female hamster?"

"How am I supposed to bond with some random female? I need to find someone of like mind with similar interests."

"Right? And how are you going to do that?"

"I plan to register with Rodent Match."

"Is that some sort of dating agency?"

"Precisely. It's a dating agency specifically for rodents. They cover all the rodents, but there's quite an active hamster contingent on there from what I understand."

"Is it available on RodentNet?"

"No, more's the pity. Although they have a very good reputation, they're a little behind the times technology-wise. It's all very old fashioned; very old school. I'll need you to get me an application form."

"For Rodent Match?"

"Yes. Everything Rodent has the forms. They act as an agent for Rodent Match. Will you pop in there, pick one up, and let me have it as soon as possible? Then I can get the ball rolling."

"Sure. Why not?"

When I got downstairs, I'd expected to find a cup of tea waiting for me. Instead, Aunt Lucy ushered me into the hallway.

"Jill, do you mind if we go out for a drink? I think Lester wants to make a few phone calls. He's job hunting. It would probably be better if you and I weren't here."

"No problem. Do you want to go to Cuppy C?"

"Oh, goodness no! I see enough of the twins as it is. They're always coming around here. There's another coffee shop I often go to in Candlefield. It's probably my favourite."

"You'd better not let the twins hear you say that."

"It's called Holo."

"That's an unusual name. As in, an empty space?"

"No, not H-O-L-L-O-W. It's H-O-L-O. Short for hologram."

"I'm intrigued."

Holo was some distance outside of Candlefield city centre. It was obviously very popular because when we got there, we only just managed to grab a table.

"I don't get the significance of the name?" I looked around, still trying to work it out.

"Do you see the two people behind the counter?"

"Yeah?"

"They're holograms."

I did a double take. "Really?"

"They're very good, aren't they?"

"Unbelievably good. I would never have known."

"If you look very closely, you can tell when they move."

I stared at them for several minutes, and sure enough,

when they moved, they seemed to flicker a little.

"How does it work? How do they take orders and serve customers?"

"No one knows. The people behind Holo are a bit of a mystery. No one seems to know who they are. Somehow, they managed to concoct a spell which allows the holograms to interact with real objects. For example, they can pick up and carry things. And they take money at the till."

"That's amazing."

"I know. I love it. And every time you come here, the holograms are different. You never see the same ones twice."

Aunt Lucy wanted to pay, but I insisted it was my turn.

What do you mean, it's about time?

"Could I have a pot of tea for two, please?" I asked the hologram behind the counter.

"Green tea? Fruit tea?"

"Earl Grey, please. And a couple of those cupcakes."

The hologram took my money. "We'll bring them over to your table."

I'd always thought that the whole point of holograms was that they weren't real. But the ones in Holo were some sort of hybrid human/hologram thing. It was all much too complicated for my simple mind.

A few minutes later, one of the holograms brought our order over. He served us with a smile, and unlike Jules, managed not to spill anything.

"This is really strange," I said to Aunt Lucy. "Are you sure they're holograms?"

"Why else would the shop be called 'holo'?"

We eventually got onto the subject of the twins' plans to

expand into Washbridge.

"I'm not sure about it," she said. "I think they may be biting off more than they can chew."

"They seem really keen on the idea."

"That's just it. You know how they are. They get a bee in their bonnet, and they dive in feet first. They don't think it through. You should know that better than most; you witnessed the chocolate fountain and conveyor belt debacles. But this, this is serious money. If it goes wrong, it could have a knock on effect on Cuppy C. I don't suppose you could try to make them see sense, could you?"

"I've got even less chance of doing that than you have. Every time they come up with a brainwave, I try to talk them out of it, but they take no notice. If they've got their hearts set on it, I doubt anything I say will make a difference. What I don't understand is where the money is coming from. They've only recently bought their houses. It's going to cost them a pretty penny to open a shop in Washbridge."

"I know." Aunt Lucy frowned. "I asked them, but they fobbed me off. I think they must be borrowing it, and that's what really worries me. Still, they're both adults now. There's nothing you or I can do about it. We'll have to keep our fingers crossed that it works out."

Just then, a woman on the opposite side of the shop started laughing so loudly that everyone began to stare at her. What on earth was she laughing at? She was at a table by herself, and didn't appear to be reading, or even looking at her phone. She was laughing uncontrollably for no apparent reason. The strange thing was, she didn't look happy. In fact, she seemed quite distressed.

The laughing continued. She was getting redder and redder in the face.

"Is she okay?" Aunt Lucy said.

"I don't know."

Then the woman stood up and reached out, as though she was asking for help. Before anyone could react, she knocked over the table as she slumped to the floor. Only then, did the laughter stop.

"Quick, somebody, call an ambulance," the man kneeling beside her yelled.

One of the holograms reached for the phone, and made a call to the emergency services.

"Is she okay?" someone shouted.

The man kneeling beside her looked up, and shook his head.

***

I called the number shown on the advert for the missing dog. The man who answered obviously thought I'd found his dog, and was rather disappointed when I said I hadn't. I asked if I could go over to his place to talk to him. He wasn't keen, but I managed to persuade him in the end.

Boris Froggatt was a plump, middle-aged man with red cheeks.

"I don't suppose Hector's turned up yet, has he?" I asked.

"I'm afraid not. Yours is the only phone call I've had so far. I had hoped the advert in the Bugle might generate some interest. It cost enough. But so far, nothing."

"What exactly happened, Mr Froggatt?"

"Hector was in the garden. It had never occurred to me that anyone would want to steal him. There's a fence all the way around, but it's not particularly high. Someone could climb over it fairly easily. Hector's only a small dog; he doesn't weigh much. And he's very friendly; he wouldn't snap or bark at anyone. He'd probably just lick their hands as they picked him up. I can only think that somebody must have climbed over the fence, and passed Hector to an accomplice on the other side. Horrible people. I don't know how they can live with themselves."

"Look, this may seem a strange question, Mr Froggatt, but was Hector wearing anything of any value?"

"How do you mean?"

"Like a collar with jewels on it, for example?"

"No. Hector didn't really like wearing any kind of collar. But of course he had to for his name disc. I bought him a very lightweight fabric one."

"And the dog himself? Had he won any shows?"

"No. He's just a mutt, but I love him to bits."

Chapter 6

Jack wasn't in when I got home from the office. I was standing in the kitchen, looking out of the back window, when I noticed there were three—no four—wait, five mounds of soil in the middle of the lawn. What was going on?

I went outside to check. Mrs Rollo was in her back garden.

"Hi, Jill."

"Hello, Mrs Rollo."

She followed my gaze.

"Oh dear. It looks like the mole is back."

"Mole?"

"We get a lot of moles around these parts. Didn't you know?"

"No, I don't remember seeing that on the estate agent's details. It said, 'Small lawn to rear,' not, 'Small lawn with moles to rear.' How do I get rid of it?"

"Don't ask me. I've had my fair share of moles too. I've tried everything, but I can't get rid of the pesky little things. I've given up."

"But it's spoiling my lawn."

"I know, but what can you do?"

I made my way back inside. Mrs Rollo might have given up the battle, but I was determined not to let a mole spoil my lawn.

"Don't get comfortable out there, Mr Mole," I shouted at the window.

"Who are you talking to?"

I hadn't heard Jack come in.

"To the mole."

"You're talking to a mole?"

"Yeah." I pointed. "Look at all those molehills."

"Moles are such sweet little creatures."

"Sweet? There's nothing sweet about it. It's spoiling our lawn. If I get hold of it, it won't be sweet for very long."

"Don't forget it's your turn to cook," he said.

"It can't be. I cooked yesterday."

"No you didn't. I did. Don't you remember? We had chicken arrabiata."

"Oh, yeah." Drat—his memory was far too good. "I have an idea. Why don't we get a takeaway?"

"Okay—if you're paying."

"We should split it."

"No chance. It's your turn to cook. If you can't be bothered, then you have to pay."

So mean.

I grabbed my phone, and pulled up a listing of local takeaways. I was used to living in and around Washbridge town centre where there were any number of places to get a takeaway. But here in Smallwash, there were only four to choose from.

"That one looks promising," Jack said, looking over my shoulder.

"One Minute?"

"Yeah."

"Have you seen what it says?" I clicked on the link. "Look at this: *'We'll get your takeaway to you in one minute or your money back.'* How can anybody possibly promise that?"

"That's what it says, so why not take them up on it?" Jack said. "What do we have to lose? Either we get the food really quickly, or it doesn't cost anything."

"You're so gullible, Jack. Don't you realise there'll be small print somewhere that gives them a get-out?"

"I think we should give it a go."

"Okay. On your head be it."

We both chose something from the menu. I went for ribs; Jack went for curry. The app was easy to use. After we'd made our selection, I paid by card and pressed 'Place Order.'

I checked my watch. "It's six fifty-three, I'll be surprised if it gets here before—"

There was a knock at the door. Jack gave me a smug look.

"Don't be ridiculous. It must be Megan or Mrs Rollo. It can't be the food." I went to answer the door, leaving Jack in the kitchen.

Standing there, was a man wearing a white t-shirt with the logo of a clock, and underneath it the words, *'One Minute or Your Money Back.'*

"Is this the Gooder residence?"

"Yeah?"

"I have your order. Ribs and curry?"

"You're a wizard, aren't you?" I said in a whisper.

"Busted." He smiled. "And you're a witch."

"Shush! My husband's through there. No wonder you can deliver in one minute. You're using magic."

"Of course I'm using magic. How else do you think I could do it?"

"What about the Rogue Retrievers?"

"So far no one's cottoned on. There aren't many sups around here—there's the guy across the road, and a vampire a couple of streets away. The humans don't care or even notice as long as they get their food quickly. You won't say anything, will you?"

"Me? No, I won't say a word."

"Thanks. I'm Malcolm, by the way."

"Jill."

"Pleased to meet you, Jill. Enjoy your meal."

"Wow!" Jack said, when I brought the food through. "However did they do that?"

"Who cares? Just as long as the food's good."

I'd no sooner started on my ribs than my phone rang. It was Kathy.

"Have I caught you in the middle of eating?"

"How did you know?"

"Because it sounds like you've got a mouthful of food."

"We got a takeaway."

"Are you made of money? Let me guess, it was your turn to cook."

"I don't remember whose turn it was."

"Liar!" She laughed. "Anyway, I rang to tell you that I asked Pete if Sebastian and Jethro have girlfriends. Sebastian does, but Jethro doesn't. And what's more, Jethro had already asked Pete about your new P.A."

"Are you sure it was her he was asking about?"

"I think so. He said it was the girl who was with a guy with acne."

"That's Jules."

"It seems Jethro was quite taken with her, so maybe we can play Cupid."

"Great. I'll tell Jules. By the way, did Megan come over to your place?"

"Don't mention that woman to me."

"I take it she did, then."

"Yes, and she brought me flowers—trying to butter me

up, no doubt. It didn't work though. I stayed in the room with them all the time she was here. Pete kept saying I didn't need to be there, but I wasn't shifting. I don't trust her."

"She actually seems quite nice."

"Yeah, they all do. I've told you, Jill, keep an eye on her. Don't leave her alone with Jack."

"But it went okay, did it?"

"I think so. She seemed happy enough when she left."

***

The next morning, I set off for work before Jack. When I got to the toll bridge, the man in the booth took my money, then said, "Are you Jill by any chance?"

"Yeah."

"I thought so. A friend of yours asked me to have a word with you."

"A friend?"

"Mr Ivers."

"Oh?" That *friend*. "How did you know it was me?"

"He told me which model of car you drove, and said that I'd know it because it was always dirty."

Cheek! I'd only washed it last month—or the month before that. Definitely within the last six months.

"Anyway, he said to tell you he's sorry he won't be seeing you as often because he's been transferred to the office. He'll make sure you still get your copy of the newsletter though. He said he'll let me have it, so I can give it to you, and collect the money."

"Great. That's *really* great! Thanks very much."

As I drove into Washbridge, I noticed that a couple of

the billboards at the side of the road had large adverts for Ever A Wool Moment. I was used to seeing the adverts on the buses and taxis, but it seemed Grandma had now extended her reach even further. That woman was a marketing genius.

When I arrived at work, Mrs V gestured to my office. "Your grandmother is waiting for you. I tried to get her to wait out here, but she didn't take any notice of me."

Grandma was sitting in *my* chair—at *my* desk. Winky was hiding under the sofa, as he always did when she was around.

"What's going on behind that screen?" Grandma pointed. "It looks like someone's building something."

"It's an old copying machine. The man said it needs a new part."

I could hardly tell her it was Winky's time machine, could I? She already thought I had a few screws loose because I'd turned down the chance to move to level seven.

"So, Grandma, what brings you here at this early hour?"

"It maybe early to you, young lady. I've been up since five o'clock. I want to talk to you about the twins. Have a seat."

"Are the girls all right?"

"That's a matter of opinion, but, yes, I suppose so."

"So what's wrong?"

"I assume you've heard about their latest hare-brained scheme?"

"You mean the shop across the road from Ever?"

"Yes. What are they thinking? They can barely make

Cuppy C pay, and they have no experience of working and living among humans. It's a totally different ball game."

"So it's not that you're annoyed because they're going to be competition for your tea room?"

"Don't be ridiculous. The twins, competition for me? No, I'm worried for them. Nobody's told me anything, as usual, but from what I can gather, they'll have to borrow money to finance this madcap idea. What happens when it all goes pear-shaped? They'll probably end up losing Cuppy C. Then where will they be?"

"Have you talked to them about it?"

"I've tried, but you know how it is with young people. They have no respect for their elders. That's why I came to see you. For some reason, and goodness knows why, they're far more likely to listen to you than me. So I thought you could have a word, and make them see the folly of their ways."

"What makes you think they'll listen to me? I tried to persuade them not to invest in the conveyor belt. Did they listen? Of course not. I might as well have talked to this brick wall."

"Well, you have to try. You need to change their minds because this could be disastrous."

"Okay, Grandma, I'll see what I can do, but I don't hold out much hope."

She stood up. "Oh, and I'm pleased to see you got that awful sign of yours changed."

"Do you like the new one?"

"It's certainly an improvement. At least this one doesn't make it look like you're running a tanning salon."

***

I found it curious that two dogs should go missing in such a short period of time. But then, it wasn't really a subject I was familiar with, so maybe it wasn't so unusual. I decided the best way to find out was to check the archives of The Bugle. Fortunately, I was able to do that at Washbridge library, and didn't need to go to The Bugle's offices. I had no desire to bump into Dougal Bugle and his merry men.

On The Bugle's website, I clicked on the archive link, and then searched on 'missing dog' and 'lost dog', and every other combination I could think of. It turned up very few results. That didn't necessarily mean that dogs didn't go missing in Washbridge, but that such disappearances weren't newsworthy.

In fact, the only hits in the last five years were the recent advert that Boris Froggatt had placed for his missing dog, and an article from four years earlier. The older article wasn't specifically about a missing dog—it was a front page article about the murder of a Mr Lewis. The search had thrown up that article because it mentioned that Mr Lewis had been a little down on the days just before his murder because his dog had gone missing.

My P.I. curiosity was piqued. After performing further searches on the name of Joseph Lewis, it became clear that his murderer had never been brought to justice, even though the police had found what they believed to be his DNA on the victim's clothing. Still, that wasn't my concern. I was meant to be finding a missing dog, and it was quite obvious that I wasn't going to get any *leads* from The Bugle archives.

Leads? Get it? Come on, that was funny! Sheesh!

Chapter 7

It was time for my first appearance at the Combined Sup Council. As with many other Candlefield organisations, they met in the town hall. Tabitha Hathaway was waiting for me on the steps outside.

"Hi, Jill, are you nervous?"

"I am a little. I'm not really sure what to expect."

"Don't feel any pressure to contribute straight away. Use the first few meetings to get to know people, and to see how we operate."

She led me inside, and into the meeting room where everyone was already seated.

"As you already know, we have a new member joining us today. Jill Gooder was responsible for ridding Candlefield of TDO—something I'm sure we're all grateful for. So, everyone, please make Jill welcome."

I'd heard the Combined Sup Council referred to as 'the elders,' and I could see why. I was the youngest person in the room by at least twenty years, maybe more. Many of them looked even older than Grandma. There were all types of sup seated around the table: two vampires, two wizards, three werewolves, a goblin and various others. Curiously, there was only one other witch: a really old lady seated next to me. She introduced herself as Esme Duff, but when I tried to make conversation with her, I found it practically impossible. She was as deaf as a post. How she was going to contribute to the meeting, I couldn't imagine. Grandma had told me that witches were under-represented on the council, and I could see what she meant.

The meeting turned out to be dreadfully boring. We

spent the first thirty minutes poring over the minutes from the previous meeting, at which nothing had happened, apparently. Then, when the meeting-proper actually started, we spent the next fifteen minutes discussing the state of the drains in Candlefield market square. Some people felt very strongly about the situation.

"It's a disgrace," Charlie Baxter, one of the werewolves, said. "An absolute disgrace. In the northern corner of the square, there's always a puddle. It doesn't matter what the weather is like. It might not have rained for a week, but there'll still be a puddle there. Something needs to be done about it, and sharpish."

The last item on the agenda was a discussion on whether the council should recommend an increase to the budget for Rogue Retrievers. At last, this was a subject where I felt I could make a contribution. I knew how stretched Daze normally was—although it had been a little quieter recently, since all the wicked witches had disappeared.

It seemed obvious to me that an increase to the budget could only be a good thing. Unfortunately, no one seemed to share my view.

"They already get too much money as it is," one of the wizards shouted. "What do they spend it all on?"

"May I say something?" I raised my hand, and everyone turned to look at me. "I regularly work with one of the Rogue Retrievers, and I can tell you that their workload is horrendous. I'm sure that an increased budget would be of great benefit."

The discussion continued, and eventually a vote was taken. Three people voted with me, but the rest voted against. There would be no budget increase for Daze and her colleagues.

"Right," Tabitha said. "That concludes everything on the agenda. Unless there's any other business, we'll call it—"

I raised my hand again. Everyone around the table looked surprised. Perhaps they didn't generally bother with any other business.

"Jill, did you want to say something?"

"Yes, there's one subject I'd like to raise, and that's the question of the internet."

"What about it?" an elderly wizard said.

"Don't you think it's time the internet was introduced to Candlefield? It's everywhere else."

"That may be," the goblin said. "But we don't want any new-fangled inventions here in Candlefield."

"Hear, hear. Hear, hear."

"Why do we need the internet?" a female werewolf said.

"It's just a gimmick," someone else said.

A quick vote was called for, and I was in a minority of one. It made me wonder if anyone at the table had ever ventured to the human world. Had they ever actually used the internet? I had a strong suspicion the answer to both of those questions was 'no.' No wonder they'd always blocked any suggestions that the internet should be introduced to Candlefield. Alan, William, and Hamlet were all going to be very disappointed. I intended to continue to push the issue, but I was probably fighting a losing battle.

When the meeting broke up, I felt as though I'd achieved nothing. I wasn't impressed by the council. They desperately needed some young blood on there—people with new and exciting ideas. This lot were too stuck in their ways.

I'd promised Hamlet that I'd pick up an application form for Rodent Match from 'Everything Rodent.' I hadn't visited the shop for a while, but just as before, Bill Ratman was behind the counter.

"I know you, don't I?" he said. "I never forget a face."

"Jill Gooder. I have a hamster, Hamlet."

"Oh yes, I remember. Let me think now—you bought some dumbbells for him."

"That's right, yes."

"How is he getting on with those?"

"I'm not sure he's actually using them. I can't say I've noticed any difference in his appearance."

"He's probably got bored with them. A lot of hamsters buy weights, and are full of good intentions, but they soon get fed up. It's the same with Rodent Gym membership. So, what can I do for you, today?"

"I'm after an application form for Rodent Match, please."

"You're out of luck, I'm afraid."

"Why's that?"

"Rodent Match haven't sent me any for a while, and I've run out."

"I can't tell Hamlet that; he'll be devastated. Is there nothing you can do?"

"I can give you the address of Rodent Match, if you like. You could go around there to see if you can get one. If you do, perhaps you'd bring some back for me?"

Rodent Match was based at thirty-one Chinchilla Road, which was a fifteen-minute walk from Everything Rodent.

When I got there, the whole street was full of very small offices with very small doors. Presumably, all of the businesses there were run by rodents. I knocked on the door of number thirty-one.

"Come in," a tiny voice shouted.

I had to shrink myself to get through the door. Once inside, I found a dormouse behind a desk.

"Hello there." He smiled. "We don't get many witches in here. Is there something I can help you with?"

"I've just been to Everything Rodent to pick up an application form for Rodent Match."

"I'm very sorry, but *you* can't join. Rodent Match is strictly for rodents."

"The form isn't for me. It's for my hamster, Hamlet."

"Doesn't he run a book club?"

"That's him, yes."

"I'm afraid you're out of luck."

"But Bill Ratman at Everything Rodent said you'd have some."

"Normally we would, but the ink has run out on the laser printer. I'm waiting for a new toner cartridge."

"Where's that coming from?"

"Everything Rodent. If you could pop back down there and get me one, I could print some forms. I've got an account with him, so you wouldn't need to pay."

"Right." I sighed. "Okay."

Another fifteen-minute walk later, and I was back at Everything Rodent where I collected a toner cartridge from Bill Ratman. Then I made the return journey to Rodent Match, where I waited until the dormouse had printed off the application forms.

"There you go. There's about a hundred of them there.

Take one for yourself, and then if you could drop the rest in at Everything Rodent, that would be great."

"Sure. No problem. Thanks."

This time it took twenty minutes to make my way back to Everything Rodent because I was shattered.

"You look tired," Bill said.

"I'm exhausted. I've spent the last hour walking backwards and forwards between here and Rodent Match. Here are the application forms."

"Thank you. Don't forget to take one for Hamlet."

I was on my last legs when I got back to Aunt Lucy's. There was no one home, so I let myself in, and made my way upstairs. Barry came bouncing over to me.

"Can we go for a walk, Jill? Jill, can we go for a walk? I love to walk. Can we go now?"

"I'm sorry, Barry, I can't take you right now. I'm too tired."

"Aw, Jill, please."

"Aunt Lucy will take you out later. Here, have some Barkies." I threw him a handful, and that seemed to satisfy him.

"Hello again, Jill." Hamlet looked surprised to see me. "What brings you back so soon?"

"I've got the application form for Rodent Match, just like you asked."

"You shouldn't have bothered. I've changed my mind. Females are more trouble than they're worth." He gave me a puzzled look. "Are you feeling okay? You've gone awfully red in the face."

***

I'd only just got back to the house, when there was a knock at the door. Was it Mrs Rollo with yet another one of her baking masterpieces? Or Megan, wanting yet more information from Peter? Worse still, it could be Mr Hosey.

Whoever it was, knocked again.

"Jen?"

"Do you have a minute, Jill?"

"Sure. Come on in. Are you okay?" She looked a little stressed.

"I've been a nervous wreck ever since I asked you to check on Blake. I realise it's only been a couple of days, but I have to know if you've found anything?"

Little did Jen know that I hadn't been keeping tabs on Blake at all. He and I had agreed that I'd pretend to follow him, just to put Jen's mind at rest.

"There's nothing to report. I've followed him as promised, but he hasn't done anything out of the ordinary."

She breathed a sigh of relief. "So he's not seeing anyone?"

"No, nothing like that."

"I feel bad now. That I doubted him. It's just that I couldn't shake the feeling there was something he was holding back from me."

"I'm sure there's nothing. Blake loves you."

"I know. I'm just being silly."

She took my hand in both of hers.

"Thanks very much, Jill. You don't know how much this means to me."

"I take it you don't want me to keep following him?"

"I know this sounds terrible, but maybe you could continue, just for another couple of days. That way, I'll know for certain."

"Are you sure?"

"Yes. It'll be money well spent, and then I can put all this behind me, and we can get on with our lives."

"Okay, I'll be happy to."

"Thanks. I'd better go. I want to be home before Blake arrives. You won't mention any of this to him, will you?"

"No, of course not."

I hated being put in that position. I felt I had to support Blake because he was a fellow sup, but I didn't like lying to Jen. She was such a nice person. Then I had a brainwave. If I actually *did* follow Blake—just for a few hours—I'd be able to tell Jen that I'd been tailing him, and I wouldn't be lying. I had nothing booked for the next morning, so decided that's what I'd do.

When Jack came in a couple of hours later, he was in a foul mood. Every time I spoke to him, he snapped my head off.

"What's the matter with you?" I snapped back.

"Nothing."

"Don't give me that, Jack. You've been like a bear with a sore head ever since you walked in. I don't know what's happened at work, but don't take it out on me."

"I'm sorry." He sighed. "You're right. It's not your fault."

"Are you going to tell me what happened?"

"I had to go back to Washbridge station today. It's one of the cases I worked on, which is still ongoing. They needed my input, so rather than spend hours on the phone, my old gaffer asked if I'd come over to brief the new guy and his team."

"Leo Riley?"

"None other."

"Is he the one who's rubbed you up the wrong way?"

"Yeah."

"What did he do?"

"I don't really want to get into it."

"Tell me! What did he do?"

"If you must know, he was bad-mouthing you."

"What did he say?"

"That he's only been in Washbridge for five minutes, but he seems to trip over you at every turn. He said it was my fault for allowing you to get involved with cases on my watch."

"What did you say?"

"I told him if he didn't shut his mouth, I'd punch him."

I laughed. "I'm not sure that's a good idea."

"No, but think how much better I'd feel."

"I appreciate you sticking up for me, but you don't have to fight my battles. I'm quite capable of handling Leo Riley."

"I know you are. And to be honest, I hope you give him as much grief as you possibly can."

"I'll do my best." I pulled him towards me. "You're so sweet, trying to look out for me. There must be some way I can show my gratitude."

"What about these dishes?"

"They can wait."

Chapter 8

Jack was up and out, bright and early the next morning. When I eventually did stir, I immediately remembered Jen's visit from the night before. After I'd showered and dressed, I checked through the front window. Jen's car had gone, but Blake's was still there.

Ten minutes later, when he set off for work, I hurried outside, jumped in my car and followed him. Blake had told me where he worked, when we were chatting at the housewarming party, so I pretty much knew the route he'd be taking. I stayed several cars behind him. Thankfully, there were no delays at the toll bridge. When he was about three miles outside Washbridge, he took a right turn, which caught me off guard; I'd been expecting him to carry straight on. Perhaps he knew a shortcut I didn't.

After no more than a mile, he suddenly pulled up. There was a young woman standing at the side of the road. She'd obviously been waiting for him. After she'd climbed into the passenger seat, he drove off. Perhaps it was a co-worker who he gave a lift to each day. I half expected him to do a U-turn to get back on the main road, but instead he carried straight on.

Eventually he turned onto the Speedlink Industrial Estate, which was full of relatively new industrial units. He pulled up outside one called Pring Springs. I stayed about a hundred metres up the road. It was difficult to see from that distance, but it looked as though the two figures inside the car leaned towards one another. Were they kissing?

Oh bum!

Once the young woman had gone inside the building, Blake turned the car around, and drove back off the estate. I followed him. This time he did make his way back onto the main Washbridge road, and to his place of work. I carried on to my office.

That was all I needed! It had never, for a minute, occurred to me that Blake might actually be seeing someone behind Jen's back. When she'd mentioned her concern that he was keeping something from her, I'd automatically assumed it was because he had to hide the fact that he was a wizard. That was why I'd sided with him, and why I'd offered to pretend to follow him. But now, I was really concerned—what exactly had I just seen? Could it have been perfectly innocent? Had he simply been giving a lift to a friend? Or was there something more to it? I had no choice now; I had to find out what was really going on.

"Morning, Jill," Jules said when I walked into the office. I was miles away, still thinking about Blake.

"Morning, Jules. I see you're knitting again."

"I'm getting much faster. Look." She held up the scarf of many widths.

"Very nice, Jules. Very nice."

"I'm going to knit some socks next."

"You don't think that might be a little ambitious?"

"I don't think so. Look how quickly I've done this scarf."

"Yes, well, anyway, I've got something to tell you. I spoke to Peter last night."

"About Jethro and Sebastian?"

"Yeah. Unfortunately, Sebastian does have a girlfriend."

Her face fell.

"But, the good news is that Jethro doesn't."
"Oh?" She was smiling again.
"And there's even better news."
"What's that?"
"Apparently, Jethro asked about you after the housewarming."
"About me? Are you sure it was me, and not that Megan what's-her-face, your next-door neighbour?"
"It was definitely you. He specifically said the young woman who was with the guy with bad acne."
"That does sound like me. What do you think I should do? Should I contact him? Do you have his phone number?"
"That's the last thing you should do. Take it from someone who is something of an expert when it comes to the opposite sex."
What? Why are you lot laughing?
"The trick is to play hard to get."
"How do you mean?"
"If you ring him now, he'll have the upper hand. But if Peter just happens to mention that you're now single, and Jethro comes chasing after you, then you'll have all the power."
"I don't really want the power. I just want a boyfriend."
"Trust me on this, Jules. It never fails."
"Okay. As long as you're sure?"
"Absolutely sure. You're talking to the master."
When I walked through to my office, I could hear Winky hard at work behind the screen.
"How's it coming along, Winky?"
"Nearly there. Another few days, and it should be finished."

"What are you really building?"

"I've already told you. It's a time machine."

"Why don't you just pay up, and concede that this is never going to work."

"I don't think so. When it's finished, I'll give you a demonstration, then you'll have to apologise for ever doubting me."

"Yeah. Whatever."

Halfway through the morning, Jules put through a call from Maisy Topp.

"Maisy, I'm afraid I don't have any news for you, yet."

"That's okay. Toto is back home."

"Really? How?"

"Someone found him roaming the streets, and checked the address on his collar."

"That's great news."

"Please post me your bill, and I'll pay it straightaway."

Before I could say anything else, she'd hung up.

Something was bothering me about Maisy's telephone call. It was her tone—she should have sounded overjoyed at having her dog back, but instead she'd sounded rather subdued. I called Boris Froggatt.

"It's Jill Gooder. I came to see you the other day."

"I remember."

"I wondered if you'd had any luck tracing your dog?"

"Yes. He's back home."

"That's great news. Did someone find him?"

"No, he just turned up at the door."

"I see."

How very strange. Two missing dogs. Two frantic

owners. And then within the space of twenty-four hours both dogs suddenly reappear? Way too much of a coincidence for my liking.

***

The sudden, loud sound made Winky jump off the sofa and hide underneath it. It was music; incredibly loud music. Jules came rushing in.

"What on earth is that, Jill?"

"It sounds like it's coming from next door. I'd better take a look."

I made my way out of the office and along the landing. The building work looked as though it was more or less finished. There was only one workman still there, and he seemed to be tidying up. They'd knocked three small offices into one large room, and sealed up two of the old doors.

The remaining door was open, so I went inside. The transformation was incredible. The room was full of equipment: cross trainers, rowing machines, treadmills and any number of loose weights. The music was blaring out of speakers which were located along the walls on all sides. The noise was deafening.

At the far side of the room, Brent and George were working out on a couple of cross trainers. They hadn't seen me come in, and they certainly hadn't heard me.

When I was only a few feet away, they finally spotted me.

"Jill!" George shouted.

"Hiya!" Brent shouted even louder.

I put my hands to my ears, and pointed to the speakers.

"Can you turn it down?"

George picked up a remote, and lowered the volume to a much more reasonable level.

"Come to check out our new place, Jill?"

"Not really. I can't hear myself think next door with that music."

"Oh, right. Sorry about that." Brent didn't look very sorry.

"Are you sure we can't persuade you to let us have your office?" George said. "It would be ideal for a sauna."

"I've been through all this before with my previous neighbours. It was my father's office for many years, and it holds very dear memories for me. If it was just any old office, then maybe you could persuade me, but I'm not giving up Dad's old office. And I don't expect to have to put up with that level of noise from in here."

"Of course not," Brent said. "When we're open, we shan't have the music up so loud, because people will want to talk. We'll keep the volume down to a reasonable level."

"I hope so. I don't want to have to go to Zac with this."

"There'll be no need for that." George assured me. "You'll see. You'll hardly know we're here."

While I was there, I decided to get something else off my chest.

"Jules tells me you've been trying to poach her to come and work for you?"

"Every time we see Jules, she always looks bored. When I popped my head into your office the other day she was knitting. She's a young woman! She should be working in a vibrant organisation! Not in some dowdy old office. No offence."

'No offence'?

"You know what I mean?" he continued. "Don't you think she'd benefit from working somewhere more 'now'?"

"I'll have you know that my business is very 'now'."

They both grinned.

"Jules is quite happy where she is, so I'd appreciate it if you didn't make any more approaches to her."

"We won't," George said. "We've sorted out a receptionist now. We've just got to recruit a few additional instructors."

"How's everything else coming along?"

"The building work's finished, and most of the equipment has been installed. We're pretty much good to go."

"I assume you'll be opening soon then?"

"Yeah, not long now. We haven't finalised a date, but it's going to be within the next couple of weeks. There's still time for you to take advantage of the early bird membership offer. It's fifty percent off if you sign up before opening day. If you do, we can get you in shape in no time."

Get me in shape? Cheek!

Chapter 9

I wasn't looking forward to it, but I knew I'd better talk to the twins to see if I could change their minds about taking on the shop in Washbridge. I didn't fancy my chances, but if I didn't at least try, I'd have Grandma on my back again.

When I magicked myself over there, I found them sitting at a corner table. They were staring down at their drinks, and looked rather unhappy.

"What's wrong, girls?"

"Nothing," Amber said.

"Obviously, something is."

"You know that shop we were going to open in Washbridge?" Pearl looked up from her cup. "The one opposite Grandma's wool shop."

"Yeah?"

"Someone beat us to it. We got a call today to say it had already been let."

"That must be disappointing."

"It would have been great," Amber said. "We were going to take turns working in the two shops. We would have had the best of both worlds."

"That's a real shame. I thought it was a great idea," I lied.

"Grandma didn't." Amber finished the last of her coffee. "She was dead set against it."

"It's just not fair," Pearl said.

"We can still look for somewhere else." Amber was obviously trying to put on a brave face. "There must be lots of other empty shops in Washbridge."

"I guess so." Pearl shrugged. "We'll just have to keep

looking."

"Are you sure?" I had to cut this idea off at the knees. "Maybe this was a sign?"

"Absolutely sure. It might take us a while, but we'll find somewhere."

Oh bum!

Just then, a man seated by the window started laughing really loudly. Everyone looked over at him. I immediately got a sense of deja vu.

"What's with him?" Pearl said.

"I don't know."

The laughter grew louder and louder. He had the same panicked expression on his face as the woman in Holo. After a few moments, he staggered to his feet, but only managed a couple of paces before he fell to the floor. Another man, sitting close by, rushed to his side.

"Should I call an ambulance?" someone shouted.

"It's too late."

Something was definitely wrong. That was twice now that I'd seen someone start to laugh uncontrollably, and then drop dead. It was very scary.

***

I'd arranged to meet Patricia Lewis, the widow of Joseph Lewis—the man in the article I'd come across when looking through the archives for news items on lost dogs. Even though Toto and Hector had been reunited with their owners, I was still curious to learn the details of this murder.

Patricia Lewis wore her hair in a bun. She reminded me

a little of Sue Zann, the Buninator.

"Jill Gooder?" She answered the door wearing slippers.

"That's me."

"Do come in. Would you like a drink?"

"No, thanks. I've not long since had one."

We went through to the lounge, and I took a seat in the armchair. Patricia sat opposite me.

"You said you wanted to talk to me about Joseph's murder?" She picked up a woollen jumper, from the small coffee table next to the sofa, and began to squeeze it much like a child with a comfort blanket. "What do you want to know?"

"I came across an article about your husband's murder when I was researching another case. Am I right in thinking that no one has ever been charged?"

"That's right. The police have all but dropped the case. They seem to be trusting to fortune now."

"How do you mean?"

"They have the murderer's DNA. They ran a check against their databases nationwide, but there was no match. So, unless the man walks into a police station and gives himself up, the only way he's likely to be caught is if his DNA is taken in relation to some other offence. I don't hold out much hope after all this time."

"This may sound kind of weird, but I came across your husband's case when I was searching the archives of The Bugle for articles on lost dogs."

"Is that something you specialise in?"

"No. In fact, I've never had a lost dog case until recently. The article about your husband mentioned that his dog had gone missing."

"That's right. Desi—that's what we used to call him. He

was a lovely dog—a wire-haired terrier. Joseph treated him like a son, and was devastated when he went missing."

"How long was that before your husband was murdered?"

"Only a matter of days. I think there must have been a gang of dog thieves in the area because a colleague of Joseph's had her dog taken around the same time. Ironically, on the morning of the day he was killed, Joseph actually seemed much brighter. He was convinced he was going to get Desi back."

"What made him think that?"

"I don't know. He said it would be his present to himself."

"Present?"

"Didn't you know? Joseph was murdered on his birthday. He was wearing the jumper that I'd knitted for him. I'm not very good at knitting, but Joseph said he loved it. He was kind hearted like that. That was the last time I spoke to him. The next thing I heard was when the police called to tell me he'd been murdered." She pressed the jumper tight to her chest. "They gave me his clothes a few weeks later." She glanced down at the jumper. "I can't bring myself to throw this away. I had to wash it though. It was covered in dog hairs."

"Desi's?"

"Yes, and lots of others too. Joseph loved dogs. All dogs."

"You said a colleague of his also had her dog stolen?"

"Yes. She was on Washbridge Council with my husband. Now, what was her name? Charlene—Charlene West, that was it. I remember that her dog turned up again, out of the blue, the day before Joseph was murdered."

As I made my way back to the car, I remembered something that Maisy Topp had said when she'd first come to see me. She'd been in a hurry because she had a meeting—a council meeting. Coincidence? I didn't believe in them.

I called Boris Froggatt.

"You really must stop contacting me," he said. "I've told you—I have Hector back."

"I'm sorry, Mr Froggatt, I just need you to answer one quick question, please. Are you by any chance on Washbridge Council?"

"Yes. I have been for three years now."

"Thank you, Mr Froggatt. Thank you very much."

***

Jack was working late. He'd called during the day to say it would probably be close to midnight before he got in, so I'd arranged to go over to Kathy's after work. When I arrived, Peter was there.

"I didn't expect you to be home yet, Peter."

"It makes such a difference having another employee. Now I've got Sebastian *and* Jethro, we're getting through the work in a fraction of the time. Hopefully, this will become the norm."

"Speaking of Jethro, I mentioned to Jules that he might be interested in seeing her."

"What did she say?"

"She was very excited, but I told her it was probably

best to let him make the first approach—to play hard to get."

"Yeah." Kathy nodded. "That's what I always did."

Peter and I both stared at her, open-mouthed.

"What? It's true."

"I seem to remember you chased after me relentlessly until you wore me down, and I asked you out." Peter grinned.

"You never did have a particularly good memory."

"I don't have Jules's mobile phone number," I said. "But you can give Jethro my office number; he can call her on that."

Kathy had prepared pizza and chips.

"This is just what I needed, Kathy," I said through a mouth full of pizza.

"It was all I could be bothered with, to be honest. I'm shattered. You haven't forgotten it's my big day tomorrow, have you?"

"Big day?"

"I might have known you'd forget. It's my first day presenting at Wool TV."

"Oh, yeah. So it is."

"You have to watch!"

"I'll be glued to the screen." The truth was, gluing me to the screen would be the only way to get me to watch it. "What time does it go out?"

"The live broadcast is at two o'clock in the afternoon."

"Oh dear! I'll be working then."

"Don't worry, it's repeated three or four times during the day. It'll be on in the evening, so check the listings and make sure you tune in. Get Jack to watch it too, and Mrs V and Jules."

"If I do that, it will double the audience figures."

"Cheek! I'll have you know Wool TV has tens of thousands of viewers."

"Are you nervous?"

"I'm absolutely terrified, but I'm excited as well. Who knows where it might lead? I could end up on national TV."

"Probably best to walk before you run."

"Is it time yet, Mummy?" Lizzie came running in. "Is it time?"

Both kids were standing next to the table. They obviously had something on their minds.

"I think so. Auntie Jill has more or less finished her dinner, haven't you, Auntie Jill?"

"Err—yeah." What was going on?

"Lizzie and Mikey have a little surprise for you."

"Oh?" I hated surprises.

"You have to go with them, Auntie Jill."

"Right."

Lizzie grabbed one of my hands; Mikey grabbed the other. Between them, they led me to Mikey's bedroom. As soon as I walked through the door, I saw the drum on the chest of drawers, and my heart sank.

"I thought you kept your drums at TomTom, Mikey?"

"I have to keep my main drum kit there. Mum and Dad won't let me have it at home. But I still have my old drum here."

"So what's this surprise you want to show me?"

"Go and sit in the chair over there please, Auntie Jill," Lizzie said, half pushing me towards the corner of the room. Then she stood next to Mikey who had put the drum around his neck.

Oh, no! Please no! What had I done to deserve this?

"One, two, three." Lizzie counted them in.

Mikey began to thump the drum, and Lizzie began to sing. I'd never heard anything quite like it. Lizzie's voice would have shattered glass, and Mikey seemed to have no sense of rhythm.

I glanced to my left, and saw that Kathy and Peter were standing just outside the door, both of them in hysterics. I'd make them pay for this.

The torture went on for another ten minutes before the two kids took a bow. I clapped.

"That was very good, wasn't it, Auntie Jill," Kathy said, as she and Peter came into the room.

"Excellent," I said, through gritted teeth.

"Perhaps you'd like to hear another song?" Kathy grinned.

"I'd love to, but I have to get back home. I've left a thing in the thingumajig. But you were very good, Lizzie. Well done, Mikey. Keep practising." You need it.

When we got outside, I turned on Kathy and Peter.

"How could you do that to me?"

"Do what?" Little Miss Innocent said. "Surely you want to encourage your nephew and niece in their musical interests?"

"I noticed you two didn't come into the room."

"We have to listen to it all week," Peter said. "I don't see why you shouldn't have to suffer too."

***

My ears were still ringing when I got back home. It was

still light, so I looked out of the back window to see how the lawn was doing. There were two new molehills! I wasn't going to put up with this any longer. Tomorrow I'd find an expert who could tell me the best way to get rid of an unwanted mole.

Out of the corner of my eye, I spotted Mrs Rollo hard at work in her garden. Just then, I felt a vibration in my pocket. It was the Z-Call button. I hadn't heard from Z-Watch for over six months. I checked the alarm; there was a zombie somewhere in my vicinity.

Not good.

When I glanced again out of the back window, I saw them. Over the back fence, coming through the field towards Mrs Rollo's house, were two zombies.

Mrs Rollo was oblivious to the imminent danger. She was so busy watering her plants that she hadn't noticed the undead heading towards her. I had to do something, so I dashed next door.

"Mrs Rollo."

"Hello, Jill? I didn't see you there."

"Sorry. Do you remember what you said about teaching me to bake sometime?"

"I'd be happy to."

"How about now? Right now would be a really good time."

"I'm just watering the—"

"Please, Mrs Rollo. I have to bake something special for err—Jack's err—birthday. Will you help me?"

"Of course."

I glanced over her shoulder. The zombies were almost at the fence.

"Let's get inside now, shall we?"

"What about my watering?"

"Could you possibly do that afterwards?"

"I suppose so."

I ushered her inside, and slammed the door shut behind us. As I glanced through the back window, I saw the first of the zombies climbing over the fence.

Phew! That was a close call. The Z-Watch team would arrive at any minute to round up the zombies. In the meantime, I'd just have to endure Mrs Rollo's baking masterclass.

Yet another bullet I'd taken for the team.

Chapter 10

It was mid-morning the next day, and I was thinking about the missing dog case. Something about it still bothered me. I didn't even notice Mrs V come into my office.

"Jill, could you order some more paper please? I've almost run out."

"Yeah, sure. No problem."

Mrs V was just about to go back to her office when she stopped dead in her tracks. She checked her watch, then turned to me. "What have you done to it?" she said, accusingly.

"What have I done to what?"

"The cuckoo clock."

I glanced at my watch; it was dead-on ten o'clock. Precisely the time when the cuckoo should have, you know, cuckooed.

"Perhaps it needs a new battery."

"It can't need a battery, Jill. It's only been on the wall a few days. Have you broken it already?"

"Me? No!"

"Are you sure?"

"I haven't touched it." I could hear Winky laughing behind the screen. "Maybe the cuckoo got stuck," I suggested.

"I'll take a look."

"No need to bother, Mrs V. I'm sure it's fine."

"I'd rather check." She climbed onto the sofa, and opened the little door. "It isn't in here."

Oh bum!

"What isn't?"

"The cuckoo bird of course! It's gone."

"Oh yes, silly me! I'd totally forgotten. The other day when it cuckooed, the bird kind of fell out of the clock."

What? It was the best I could come up with.

"Fell out? I've never heard of that happening before."

"I thought it was a bit unusual myself. Anyway, I sent it away for repair. I haven't mentioned it before because I didn't want to upset you."

"How long will it be before it's mended?"

"Not long. Only a few days."

"I hope so, Jill. Armi would be most upset if one of the clocks that he gave me as a present had broken."

"Don't worry, Mrs V. It's all in hand. It will be as good as new in no time."

She was still tutting to herself as she went back to her office. I jumped up from my desk, and pulled back the screen.

"Where is it?"

"Where's what?" Winky was tightening a nut with his spanner.

"The cuckoo bird."

"Oh, that thing? I threw it away. It was broken."

"What do you mean, you threw it away? Where is it now?"

"Long gone. They collected the trash yesterday."

Great!

What would Mrs V do when she realised I'd broken her precious clock? I had to find a replacement bird, and quick.

***

Before I could get to the cuckoo problem, there was another pressing issue I needed to address. I'd checked the Yellow Pages, and come up with a gardening supplies and services company, which was not too far from my office. I told Mrs V that I was going out for a few minutes, and set off on foot.

The shop was called 'The Compost Heap.' It was smaller than I'd expected, but seemed to have everything one could need for the garden. The man behind the counter had a face only his mother could have loved. And only then, if you'd paid her a lot of money.

"Good morning," he greeted me. "I'm Mitchell Hole. How can I help you today?"

"I've got a problem with a mole."

"There are a lot of them about at the moment. Where is it you live, young lady?"

"In Smallwash."

"That would explain it. The moles seem to love it there. I'm not really sure why, but there are more moles per square mile in Smallwash than anywhere in a fifty-mile radius. How long have you had your mole?"

"It's difficult to say. We only recently moved into the house. It seems I inherited him."

"How many molehills do you have?"

"A lot. Around fifteen, probably. Can you help?"

"Yes indeed. You've come to the right place. We have all manner of products to rid you of that pesky little mole. To start with, we've got several brands of poison."

"Poison?"

"Or traps. We have a wide range of traps. And we have a new bit of kit, which has only just come onto the market, called 'Electromole'."

"What does that do?"
"It electrocutes the mole."
"You mean stuns it?"
"No. What would be the point of that? It kills it stone dead."
"What about the traps? Do you have a humane version?"
"Humane?" He laughed. "We don't deal in humane traps. Those moles have declared war on our gardens, so it's only right we retaliate in kind. All of our traps are designed to kill little moley. You'll generally find the mole doesn't come back once you've chopped his head off."
"I suppose not. Okay, I'll need to give it some thought."
Although I wanted rid of the mole, I didn't want to kill it. I needed to have a rethink.

As I was walking back to the office, I heard bells ringing. There was an ice cream van parked down the road. It was a hot day, and I'd been thinking about picking up a bottle of ginger beer, but an ice cream would really hit the mark.
There, behind the counter of the ice cream van, was a familiar face.
"Daze. Hi. I didn't expect to see you there."
"It's lovely and cool in here. Can I interest you in a cone? Or maybe a lollipop?"
"I'll have a cone please."
"What flavour? We have three-hundred and twenty-six."
"Really?"
"Yes. Look. There's the chart." She pointed to a laminated list of flavours, hanging from the side of the

van.

"Good gracious. What is crocodile mint?"

"Don't ask me. I just serve the stuff."

"I think I'll play it safe. I'll have two scoops. One vanilla and one strawberry, please."

"Blaze, did you get that?" Daze shouted over her shoulder.

Blaze popped his head up. "Hi, Jill."

"Hiya, Blaze. I didn't see you there."

"Jill wants a cone," Daze said. "One scoop vanilla and one scoop strawberry."

"Coming right up. What about sauce, Jill?"

"What have you got?"

"Strawberry, raspberry or chocolate."

"I think I'll have chocolate, please."

"That's three pounds twenty-five." Daze held out her hand for the cash.

"What are you two really doing here?" I asked while Blaze scooped the ice cream.

"We're after another rogue wizard. It seems to be the month for them."

"What's this one done?"

"I have to hand it to him. It's an ingenious scam he's got going. He finds properties in Candlefield where the owners are away on holiday. He shrinks their houses, and puts them inside snow globes, which he sells in Washbridge. When the poor owners come back from their holiday, they find their house has vanished."

"Has he stolen many houses?"

"Twenty-six at the last count. They fetch a good price because of how realistic they are. We've had a tip off that he's been operating in this area."

Blaze passed me my ice cream, which was smothered in chocolate sauce.

"That looks delicious." I had to lick it to stop it running down the side of the cone. "Good luck with your wizard. I'll catch up with both of you later. Bye."

***

I needed to check on Blake again. If he *was* having an affair, I was going to have strong words with him. I wouldn't be a party to his lies and deceit.

I waited across the road from his office. When he came out, I followed him on foot through the town centre. He eventually went inside one of Washbridge's newer restaurants. I hadn't been in there myself because the name had always put me off. It was called 'Grubby.' The restaurant had glass walls on three sides, so I got as close as I could without him seeing me. The maître d' took him to a table where a young woman was already seated. If I wasn't mistaken, it was the same young woman I'd seen him give a lift to the previous day. This was not looking good, but I didn't want to confront him in the middle of a busy restaurant. I'd have to get him on his own, and find out what on earth was going on.

Before leaving the office, I'd had Mrs V print out Maisy Topp's bill. I was going to deliver it by hand because I still had some unanswered questions. When I arrived at her house, she looked surprised to see me. And, if I wasn't mistaken, a little disconcerted.

"What are you doing here?"

"I was passing by, so I thought I'd drop this in." I

handed her the envelope.

"What is it?"

"Your bill."

"Do you need the money right now?"

"No. You have thirty days to pay. While I'm here, could I see Toto? I'd love to meet him."

"Toto? Err—I'm sorry. He's not here at the moment. He's at—err—my—err—sister's."

I'd never seen such an unconvincing performance. She was obviously lying, but why? Had Toto really come back? If not, why had she told me he had?

"Sorry, but I have to go. I've got things to do." She'd closed the door before I had a chance to object.

Now, my interest was really piqued, so I decided to pay another visit to Boris Froggatt.

"Oh? It's you again. Why are you here? What's this all about?"

"I wondered if it would be possible for me to see Hector."

"Oh? No, he's—err—he's not here."

"Where is he?"

"He's—err—at the groomers."

"Which one do you use?"

"Err—the one on the high street. I forget the name."

"Okay. Thank you for your time, Mr Froggatt."

Both Maisy Topp and Boris Froggatt had seemed extremely uncomfortable when I'd asked them about their dogs. It was too much of a coincidence that neither dog was home.

Something strange was going on, and I intended to get to the bottom of it.

Chapter 11

The next morning, Jack was staring through the back window at the lawn. "I thought you were going to see somebody about that mole? We've got another two molehills."

"I did. I went to a shop called 'The Compost Heap', and spoke to a man there."

"Did he have any bright ideas?"

"He had plenty of them, but they all involved killing the mole."

"Is that really necessary?"

"I don't see why. I don't want to kill it. I just want it to go somewhere else. Anyway, I've got a few ideas of my own. Give me a few days, and let me see if I can sort out this stupid mole."

"Okay, but if you need me to get involved, let me know."

"And, why would I need you to get involved?"

"You might need a man."

"To outwit a mole?" I laughed. "Yeah, I don't think so."

My phone rang. There was only one person who would call at that time of the morning.

"Jill, did you see it?" Kathy gushed. "What did you think?"

Did I see it? Did I see what? I had to think quickly.

"Jill?"

Then I remembered—her first ever appearance on Wool TV. I'd forgotten all about it.

"Yeah, it was very good. Very professional."

"You didn't watch it, did you?"

"Of course I did."

"Okay then, what was I wearing?"

"That suit of yours. The one I like."

"What was the main feature on last night's programme?"

"Okay, I admit it. I forgot, I'm sorry."

"You're unbelievable, Jill. Your only sister gets her big break, and you are so self-absorbed, that you forget to watch it."

"I said I'm sorry. I was really busy yesterday. I'm working on loads of cases at the moment."

"What about in the evening?"

"I worked late last night."

Jack grinned at me. He knew full well what he and I had been doing last night, and it *wasn't* working late.

"I'm sorry, Kathy. I'm really, really sorry."

"There's one more screening of it, tonight at seven o'clock. You'd better watch it."

"I will, I promise. How did it go?"

"Pretty good, I think. I was really nervous, but I got through it. Everybody at the station said I did really well. Pete and the kids loved it. Lizzie and Mikey have been telling everybody that their mum's on television. I thought it would be nice to hear what you thought about it too."

"I'll watch it tonight. I promise."

"All right, you'd better."

"I'm off." Jack gave me a peck on the cheek.

Once I was sure he'd gone, I double-checked that there was no one in the gardens on either side. This was my opportunity, so I slipped on some old clothes, and made my way into the back garden. I used a small trowel to scoop away the mound of soil from the newest molehill to reveal the tunnel beneath. After a final check that there was no sign of the neighbours, I shrank myself so I was small enough to get inside the tunnel. It was rather steep, and I had to hold onto the sides.

There were lots of worms, spiders and other creepy crawlies. Luckily, I had my phone with me. I used that for light, but also to flash at anything that looked as if it wanted to take a bite out of me. Eventually, the tunnel levelled off. I walked a little further until I found a second tunnel below my feet. I slid down it, and landed in a cavernous hole.

Something in front of me stirred.

"Hello." The voice came out of the dark.

I shone my light towards it.

"Hello there, Mr Mole."

"What are you doing in my house?" He stepped closer. "Who are you?"

"I'm sorry to disturb you. My name's Jill Gooder. I live above here."

"How come I can talk to you?"

"It's a bit complicated. I'm actually a witch. I used my magical powers to shrink myself, and I can talk to animals—at least some of them."

"How very unusual. I've never had the chance to talk to the two-leggeds before. I've always thought they seem to be an interesting species, even if they do choose to live above ground. Is there something I can help you with?"

"Actually, yes. Do you realise that every time you tunnel up to the surface, you leave a mound of earth, and it's rather spoiling my lawn?"

"What's a lawn?"

"It's the rectangular area of grass above here."

"I didn't realise that belonged to anyone."

"It belongs to the big building in front. That's where I live."

"I'm sorry, I had no idea. I wouldn't want to spoil your lawn."

"It's okay. I wondered if maybe you could move your home back a little, so that you're away from my garden. Maybe in the field beyond the lawn."

"I suppose so. It's all the same to me. As long as I have plenty of food, and somewhere to sleep. I don't want to be any trouble. My name's Mortimer, by the way."

"Nice to meet you, Mortimer. So you don't mind relocating, then?"

"Not at all. Let me see, you said I should move further that way?" He pointed with his front paw.

I was a little disoriented after my journey through the tunnels. "Yes—err—that's right."

"Okay, Jill. No problem. It was really nice talking to you."

"You too, Mortimer. I'd better be going."

Back at the surface, I didn't want to risk reversing the 'shrink' spell while I was on the lawn, in case anyone was around, so I waited until I was inside the house.

I was covered in soil, so I took another shower before setting off to work. Hopefully, Mortimer would be as good as his word, and I'd have no more molehills to contend with.

***

I was surprised to find both Jules and Mrs V in the office. It was supposed to be Mrs V's day off.

"Hello, you two. Are you giving Jules a knitting lesson today?"

"No. Something far more exciting," Mrs V said. "Guess what?"

"I have no idea."

"It's Wool Con soon. We're planning our visit."

"What's that?"

"A convention for all the yarnies."

"Like Comic Con?"

"Exactly!" Jules was bursting with excitement. "There'll be all sorts of stuff there: exhibitors, panels and even cosplay."

"Hang on. I can understand cosplay for things like Comic Con where people get dressed up as their favourite comic book characters. But cosplay for Wool Con?"

"Why not?" Mrs V said. "The yarnies get dressed up in all kinds of wool related costumes: Balls of wool, knitting needles—all kinds of things. It's really quite exciting, and totally crazy. I haven't been to Wool Con for years, but Jules seems very keen. We wondered if you'd mind if we both had the day off, so we can go together."

"I guess not. It's only one day."

"Why don't you come too, Jill," Jules said. "The three of us can pick a theme, and dress up to match one another."

"I don't think so. It's not really my thing."

"Please, Jill. It'll be fun."

"I'll think about it."

Jules followed me through to my office.

"Jill, can I have a word?"

"Sure. What is it?"

"It's about Jethro. I haven't heard from him yet. Are you sure playing hard to get is going to work?"

"Oh yes, take it from me. It's definitely the way to go."

"Okay. I'll just have to try to be patient."

***

After my chat with Patricia Lewis, I'd decided to take a closer look at the Bugle articles relating to her husband's murder. There was something about the whole affair that was still bugging me.

I logged onto the archive, and traced the progress of the murder investigation from the initial report when the body had been found near the canal. The police had been convinced Lewis had been murdered elsewhere, and his body dumped there. The front page of the paper that was published the day after the murder carried the headline 'Extraordinary.' I automatically assumed it would be about the murder case, but it turned out to be about a decision which had been made by the council to award a contract to a company called Tip Top Construction. Why would local politics have knocked a murder investigation off the front page? I read on, and it soon became clear that there was more than a whiff of corruption surrounding the decision. Under the contract, Tip Top would be responsible for all of the council's construction work for the next four years. The Bugle insisted the residents of Washbridge should be up in arms about the decision. There had been two other bidders for the contract—both with track records, and both well regarded. The Bugle speculated that money had changed hands because during the crucial meeting, two councillors had apparently changed their votes at the very last minute, with the result that Tip Top were awarded the multi-million-pound contract.

Judging by the date of the article, that contract would have been up for renewal again. Another coincidence? There were already far too many of them for my liking. Maybe I should take a closer look at Tip Top Construction.

***

I had to have it out with Blake, so I waited outside his office again at lunchtime. I didn't want to talk to him back in Smallwash in case Jen was around.

Just after midday, he came out.

"Blake!" I called to him.

He looked surprised to see me. "Jill, what are you doing here? It's not Jen is it? Is she all right?"

"Jen's fine. Look, there's no delicate way to say this. You know I said I was going to pretend to follow you for a few days, and then report back to Jen?"

"Yes?"

"I didn't like to lie to Jen, so I thought if I actually did follow you for a while, then I could tell her I'd tailed you without lying."

"You must be very good at your job because I never spotted you."

"Thanks. Anyway, I saw you pick up a young woman in your car, and then yesterday, I saw you having lunch with her. How am I supposed to tell Jen that everything's okay?"

"Because it is." He seemed unfazed by my revelation. "The woman you saw me with is Pamela. She's my sister. She and her husband are having a few money problems at the moment, so they've only got the one car. Some days, Pamela doesn't get to use it, so I give her a lift to work. And, occasionally we have lunch together. I can introduce you to her if you like?"

"No, that won't be necessary. I'm sorry I jumped to conclusions."

"That's okay. There's nothing going on, Jill. The only reason Jen thinks there is, is because I have to hide the fact that I'm a wizard."

"Okay, I'm glad we cleared that up. I'll report back to Jen, and let her know everything's okay. Sorry again for misjudging you."

"Don't worry about it. I can promise you that Jen is the only woman for me."

"I'd better get back to the office. I'll update Jen tonight if I get the chance."

***

That evening, the first thing I did when I got into the house, was look out of the back window to check the lawn. There were no new molehills. It looked like Mortimer had been as good as his word.

"I've been thinking," Jack said when he got home. "We should get a cat."

"What? Why on earth would you want a cat?"

"There are bound to be mice living in the field at the back. It's only a matter of time before they find their way into the house. If we had a cat, we wouldn't have to worry. Why don't you bring that ugly cat of yours home? He could live here instead of at the office."

"Winky?"

"Yeah."

"Live here?"

"Yeah. Why not?"

"No way is Winky coming to live here."

"But why?"

"He drives me insane."

"What do you mean?"

How was I meant to answer that without looking like a complete nut-job?

"He just does."

"Okay then, we'll get another cat."

"What happens if Winky finds out?"

"Sorry?" Jack looked at me as though I'd lost my mind. "What do you mean, 'if he finds out'?"

"Nothing. I'll think about it." It was time to change the subject. "Look, have you seen the back garden? There are no fresh molehills."

"Yeah, I noticed. How did you manage that?"

"I have skillz."

"What did you do?"

"I can't tell you. It's a trade secret."

Before Jack could press me further, there was a knock at the door. It was Megan.

"Are you okay, Megan?" Jack sounded a little too concerned for my liking.

"Yeah, it's nothing really. I'm just being silly."

"What is it?" I said. "Do you want to come in?"

"No, it's all right. I just wondered if either of you knew anything about moles?"

Chapter 12

"Did you watch it?" Kathy screamed at me, as soon as I answered the phone.

I was halfway through my cornflakes; Jack had already left for work.

"Watch what?"

"I knew you'd forget!"

"Oh? You mean your TV show? Of course I did."

"You forgot, didn't you?"

"No. I can prove I watched it. You were wearing a pink blouse, and you had your hair taken up into a bun."

"What was on the show?"

"There was an item on the importance of quality knitting needles. Now do you believe me?"

"Okay, sorry. What did you think of it?"

The truth was that I'd forgotten all about it again, but fortunately, Jack had remembered just in time. It was so boring that I'd fallen asleep after fifteen minutes. As long as Kathy didn't ask me about the last half of the show, I'd be okay.

"I thought you did really well, Kathy."

"You're not just saying that, are you?"

"No, honestly. I thought you were great."

"Thanks, Jill. Do you think I have a future in the business?"

"You've definitely got off to a good start. Did you enjoy it? That's the main thing."

"Yeah, I did. I was really nervous, but after a few minutes, I seemed to relax. Now, I can't wait to do it again next week."

Before going into the office, I magicked myself over to Candlefield. I'd had a phone call from Aunt Lucy. She'd asked if I'd go over and see her. I could tell she was upset about something.

"Jill, thank you so much for coming over."

"You sounded upset. Is something the matter?"

"It's a friend of mine, Gloria Cloverleaf. She's died."

"Oh dear. Had she been ill? Was it expected?"

"It came completely out of the blue. She's the same age as me, and as far as I'm aware, she'd been in perfect health."

"What happened?"

"That's just it. Apparently, she was in the supermarket doing her weekly shop, and suddenly she started laughing uncontrollably. Then she collapsed and died. Just like that."

"That sounds very much like what happened to the woman who collapsed when you and I were in Holo."

"That's what I thought."

"And I saw a man die in exactly the same way in Cuppy C, the other day."

"The twins told me someone had taken ill and died, but they didn't mention the laughing."

"It definitely sounds like the same thing. That's three we know of, but I suppose there could be others."

"What do you think is going on?" Aunt Lucy said.

"I really don't know."

"You should look into it, Jill. Do you have the time?"

"Of course."

"I'd be so grateful. Gloria was a very good friend. It would help to know how she died."

"Leave it with me."

While I was in Candlefield, I popped into Cuppy C. Amber grabbed me as soon as I walked in the door, and ushered me through to the back.

"Jill, you must promise not to tell Pearl this."

"Not to tell her what?"

"After we'd been to your housewarming party, William and me got talking. We never got around to having a housewarming party when we moved in, so we've decided to have one this Saturday."

"How are you going to keep it a secret from Pearl? Surely, you're going to invite her and Alan?"

"Yes, we'll invite them, but not until the day before. You know what she's like; she's always copying me. If I tell her sooner, she'll decide to throw one too. You have to promise you won't tell her."

"Okay."

"And, you will come, won't you, Jill?"

"I guess so."

Satisfied, Amber went skipping back into the shop.

Another housewarming party? Great! That was just what I needed. I couldn't even ask Jack to go with me, so I'd have to face it on my own. Maybe if there were enough people there, I could just show my face and sneak away.

I was about to go back into the shop when Pearl intercepted me.

"Jill, can I have a word?"

"Sure."

"Will you promise not to say anything to Amber?"

That sounded ominous. "Of course. What is it?"

"Alan and I got to talking after we'd been to your housewarming party. We enjoyed it so much that we've decided to have one too."

"When?"

"This Saturday."

Oh, bum!

"Surely, you're going to invite Amber?"

"Yes, of course, but if we tell her now, she'll probably decide to have one too. You know how she is. She's always copying me. You will come, won't you?"

"Can you just hold on there a minute, Pearl?"

"Yeah, I suppose so." She looked puzzled.

I walked back into the shop. "Amber, have you got a minute?"

She followed me into the back.

"Look, you two, there's no easy way to say this, so I'll just come straight out with it. In the last few minutes, both of you have invited me to a housewarming party this Saturday."

Amber look daggers at Pearl; Pearl returned the look.

"I thought of it first," Amber said.

"No, you didn't. I thought of it first."

"You can't have yours on Saturday. We're having ours on Saturday."

"No, you're not. We're having ours then."

"Girls! Timeout," I interrupted. "Look, it's obvious you'll both be inviting the same people. They can't be in two places at the same time, so you're going to have to come to some agreement on days."

"Ours is on Saturday," Amber said.

"No, it's not. Ours is."

"I'll leave you two to battle it out. When you've decided what you're doing, let me know."

With a bit of luck, they'd never reach an agreement, and

there wouldn't be any housewarming parties.

***

Back in Washbridge, I had an appointment with a new client. All I knew about her was her name: Jessica Lambeth. She hadn't given me any details over the phone, and when Mrs V showed her into my office, I could see that she'd been crying.

"Are you okay?"

"I'll be all right in a minute."

"Can I get you a drink?" Mrs V offered.

"Not for me, thank you."

She took a seat, and I waited until she'd composed herself. Jessica Lambeth was in her late twenties; everything about her looked sad, even her clothes.

"I don't really know how to explain this," she managed, eventually. "My boyfriend, Paul—he isn't my boyfriend."

"What do you mean? Has he ended the relationship?"

"No. We're still together. What I mean is, Paul isn't Paul. He looks like Paul, and he sounds like Paul, but it's not him."

"Perhaps he's feeling a little under the weather at the moment?"

"No, that's not it. He's started to act differently. We used to spend most evenings together, either at his place or mine. Now, suddenly he's started to go out in the evenings. He told me he's been playing snooker with a friend, but I don't believe him."

"Do you think he might be cheating on you?"

"I never thought I'd suspect Paul of anything like that, but yes, I think it's possible. That's why I'm here. I'm hoping you can find out what's going on."

"Can you give me his details?"

She gave me his name, address, and his place of work, and I promised to see what I could find out.

After Jessica Lambeth had left, I made a call to Tip Top Construction using the name Sarah Mullen.

"Hello there," I said, in my poshest voice. "I wonder if I could speak to Arthur Longstaff?"

Arthur Longstaff was the CEO of Tip Top Construction. I'd read numerous articles about the man, and none of them painted him in a good light. If the newspaper reports were to be believed, he was ruthless, and wouldn't think twice about destroying his competition in any way he could. The man was a multimillionaire, and most of his money had come from construction contracts with councils, including Washbridge. His country house was several miles outside Washbridge.

"Who's calling please?"

"Sarah Mullen from CEO Spotlight. We're doing a series of articles on a few of the most successful CEOs in the country, and I'm hoping to interview Mr Longstaff."

"I'll put you through to his Press Secretary."

The line went dead for a few minutes.

"Hello, Tamara Trotter here. I'm Arthur Longstaff's Press Secretary. What exactly is it you're after?"

"As I explained to your colleague, CEO Spotlight is doing a number of articles on the most successful CEOs in the country. I was hoping to arrange an interview with Mr Longstaff."

"I've never heard of your magazine."

"Really? It's one of the better-known magazines in the

business arena."

"If it was that well-known, I would have heard of it."

"Still, do you think I could arrange a meeting with Mr Longstaff?"

"I'm sorry, but that won't be possible. Mr Longstaff is extremely busy and never gives interviews. If you have a list of questions, you're welcome to submit them to me. If they're appropriate, I may be able to provide you with written answers. That's the best I can do."

"I was hoping for a face-to-face interview."

"Sorry. That's not possible."

The line went dead. I wasn't going to get anywhere with her.

***

Jack arrived home a few minutes after me; he came bearing gifts.

"This is for you." He handed me a small square package.

"I like it when you buy me presents."

"Yeah. I like it when you buy them for me, too. Oh, wait a minute—you never do." He grinned.

"That's not true." It so was. "What is it?"

"I saw a guy selling these, and I thought you'd love one."

I tore off the gift wrap. Inside was a plain white box which I opened quickly. It was a snow globe; a beautiful snow globe.

"Do you like it?" Jack said.

"I love it."

"Isn't it the most realistic house you've ever seen inside

a snow globe? Look at the detail. If you look through the windows, you can actually see the furniture inside."

He was right; the detail was fantastic. But, given what I knew, that was hardly surprising.

Chapter 13

The next morning, I stared in disbelief as Jack poured almost a third of a pint of milk onto his cornflakes.

"Yuk!"

"What's up?"

"How can you put so much milk on?"

"That's how I like them."

"But they're all soggy, and horrible and yukky."

"They're delicious." He shovelled a spoonful of the soggy mixture into his mouth.

"I can't think what I ever saw in you."

He grinned, as best he could with a mouth full of soggy cornflakes.

"Anyway, about that snow globe you bought me?"

He swallowed the mush. "What about it?"

"Where did you get it from?"

"No, you can't take it back to get the money."

"I don't want to take it back; I really like it."

"I know what you're like. It wouldn't be the first time you've taken one of my presents back."

"Those gloves were too small for me."

"How was I supposed to know you had enormous hands?"

"I do *not* have enormous hands, thank you. They were kids' gloves."

"Why do you want to know where I got the globe from, then?"

"I thought Kathy might like one. I was thinking of buying her one as a surprise."

"You never buy your sister a gift. Or anyone else for that matter."

"That's not true. I just don't make a big song and dance about it like you do. So, where was it from?"

"There's a guy selling them around the side of the station in West Chipping."

"The police station? He's taking a bit of a risk, isn't he?"

"Not the police station; the railway station. I doubt he has a licence, so he may not still be around."

"I might take a drive over there."

"I can pick one up for you, if you like?"

"It's okay. You wouldn't know which one Kathy would like. I'll need to choose it for her."

"Fair enough."

Daze had told me about a wizard, who was shrinking real houses in Candlefield, putting them into snow globes, and then selling them in Washbridge. It appeared he'd moved his operation to West Chipping where Jack was now stationed. Maybe the wizard had got wind that the Rogue Retrievers were after him. I'd soon find out.

Jack finished the last of the mulch, gave me a kiss on the forehead, and then left for work. As I was putting the pots into the sink, I noticed that Megan was in her garden, staring at the lawn. When I took the rubbish out to the bin, she spotted me.

"Morning, Jill."

"Morning, Megan. Are you okay?"

"Yeah, I'm on mole watch."

"Is he back again?"

"There are three more molehills this morning. I don't know where he suddenly came from."

"It's a bit of a mystery, isn't it?" Snigger.

"I think I'll have to ask at the garden centre to see what

they recommend. Or maybe I could ask Peter. Do you think he'd mind if I rang him?"

"Not at all. I'm sure he'd be happy to help."

And Kathy would be thrilled too.

Stirring it? Who, me? I wouldn't dream of it.

***

As I left the house for work, I glanced across the road. Blake's car wasn't on his drive, but Jen's was still there, so I popped over.

"Morning, Jill. Do you want to come in?"

"No thanks, I'm on my way to work. I wanted to give you the final report on Blake."

"Okay, but don't talk too loud. I don't want the neighbours to hear."

"There's nothing to tell, Jen. I've followed him for five days now, and he hasn't done anything at all suspicious. I haven't seen him so much as talk to another woman."

She sighed with relief, and then smiled. "Thank you, Jill. Thank you so much. That's really put my mind at rest."

"So you'll stop worrying about Blake holding things back from you?"

"Yes, I'll try. At least now I know nothing serious is going on. I guess everyone has their little secrets, don't they?"

"I suppose so." And a few giant ones.

"How much do I owe you, Jill?"

"Nothing. You're a neighbour. It's on the house."

"No, please, I insist. I'd feel so much better if you let me pay you."

"You can buy me lunch sometime."

"Okay, if you're sure. That's very kind."

"I'd better get going. No more worrying, Jen. Promise?"

"I promise."

Phew! I was glad that was over. Jen would probably always have the feeling that Blake was keeping something from her, but hopefully now, she wouldn't fear the worst.

***

When I got to the office, I could hear the music from next door. Jules had her earphones in, so she didn't hear me come through the door. Only when I tapped on her desk did she notice me and take out the earphones.

"Sorry, Jill, I didn't hear you come in."

"How long has that music been playing next door?"

"It was like that when I got here."

"Right. I'll have to have words with them."

Before confronting the I-Sweat guys, I thought I'd better check on Winky.

He was looking out of the window; wearing his earmuffs. He didn't realise I was there until I slapped the windowsill next to him, and then he almost fell off his perch.

"What on earth do you think you're doing?" He pulled off the earmuffs. "I almost fell."

"Sorry." I laughed.

"You look sorry. When are you going to sort out that crowd next door? That music is driving me nuts."

Just then, the music stopped.

"There, I've stopped it."

"You didn't do anything."

"Of course I did. I'm a powerful witch. I willed it to

stop, and it did." I lied.

He one-eyed me suspiciously.

By mid-morning, there had been no more sounds from next door, so I decided to give the I-Sweat guys the benefit of the doubt.

When a chill fell over the office, I thought maybe it was my dad. I hadn't seen him since his first appearance as a ghost.

"Jill! Long time, no see." It was the colonel, and by his side was Priscilla.

"Nice to see you, Colonel. You too, Priscilla. How are you both?"

"Apart from being dead?" Priscilla laughed at her own joke. "We're great."

"Absolutely top notch, Jill," the colonel said. "We have something exciting to tell you, don't we, Cilla?"

"We certainly do." Her face lit up. "Well, to show you really." She held out her hand. "Look."

"What a beautiful ring. Am I to take it that you two are engaged?"

"We are." Priscilla giggled.

"I thought it was time I made Cilla an honest woman, so I bought the ring, got down on one knee, and popped the question. And, what do you know, she said yes."

"I'm really thrilled for you both. Have you set a date?"

"Nothing firm yet. But when we do, we'll let you know because we'd like you to come to the wedding. You will come, won't you?"

Just what I needed—another wedding. "Of course. I'd love to."

"I'd like you to be my maid of honour," Priscilla said.

"Maid of honour? Right. What colour would I have to wear?"

"I thought pink would be nice."

***

The house and grounds of Arthur Longstaff's country estate were surrounded by a huge wall. It brought back memories of the first time I'd ever used the 'levitate' spell. Back then, I'd been absolutely hopeless. I'd chosen the wrong method to descend, and had landed with a thud. But now, I was much more experienced, and with my additional powers, I was able to simply glide over the wall. Once on the other side, I could see the main house in the distance. A little closer to me, behind the house, were two outbuildings. I crept up to the first one, and looked inside. It was a stables with several horses inside.

As I walked slowly towards the second building, several dogs began to bark. The door wasn't locked, so I slipped inside. It was obviously a large kennel block, which was full of dogs. As I walked down the central aisle, dogs of every shape and size watched me.

Halfway down the aisle, I spotted a dog that looked familiar. It was the one I'd seen in the advert in the Bugle. It was Hector. I walked up to the gate.

"Hector?"

He responded immediately to his name, and came running towards the gate, trying desperately to lick my face through the bars.

"I'm Hector! Have you come to take me home? Please take me home. I don't like it here."

"I will, but I need you to be quiet."

"Okay."
"I'm looking for a poodle called Toto."
"He's down there."
"Okay. Wait there. I'll be back."
Toto was still wearing his diamond-encrusted collar.
"Toto?"
"Who are you?"
"I've come to take you home."
"You have?" His tail began to wag, and he jumped up so his front paws were on the bars. "Thank you! I miss my home."
Just then, I noticed a wire-haired terrier in the kennel next to Toto. It was standing at the back, and looked rather nervous.
"Hey!" I called to it. "Come here. It's all right. I won't hurt you."
The dog walked slowly towards the gate.
"What's your name, boy?"
"Desi," he said, in little more than a whisper.
"How long have you been here, Desi?"
"A long time."
"What happened to your owner?"
He stared down at the floor.
"Desi, was your owner Mr Lewis?"
"Did you know him?" He looked up.
"Not exactly, but I was at his house the other day. I spoke to Mrs Lewis."
"Really?"
"Yes. She still misses you. Do you know what happened to Mr Lewis?"
"He came to rescue me, but then that horrible man, Longstaff, hit him with a spade. He killed him. Over

there." He gestured towards the door. "Then they took him away."

"It's going to be okay, Desi. I have to leave you here for a little while longer, but don't worry, you'll be home soon."

It would only be a matter of time before someone came to see why all the dogs were barking, so I had to act quickly. There was no way I could simply walk out with two dogs, but if I shrank them, I could put them in my pocket, and then go back the way I came.

With my additional powers, I could now shrink not only myself, but other objects and people. I shrank Hector first, so he could fit easily in the palm of my hand. His bark had become nothing more than a squeak. I slipped him gently into one of my pockets, and then did the same with Toto, putting him into my other pocket. Having those two dogs in my pockets brought back happy childhood memories of another of my collections.

Before I left, I reassured Desi that someone would be back soon to take him home.

***

Maisy Topp seemed surprised to see me.

"What are you doing here, Jill? I told you I don't need your help any longer."

"I thought maybe you'd like Toto back."

"I told you, he's already back."

"Really? Look over there." I pointed to the back seat of the car where the dogs, which had now been restored to their normal size, were looking through the window.

"Toto!" She screamed, and ran over to the car. "Are you all right, boy?"

I opened the door, and the dog leapt into her waiting arms.

Maisy was crying as Toto licked her face. While the two of them got reacquainted, I made a phone call.

"Where is he?" Boris yelled when he arrived.

He'd no sooner got the words out than Hector ran towards his owner. Yet another happy reunion.

We were all in Maisy's kitchen: me, two happy owners, and two even happier dogs.

"So when you both told me you had your dogs back, you lied," I said.

"I'm sorry about that, Jill." Maisy was tickling Toto's tummy.

"Me too." Boris nodded.

"I understand why you did it. Unless I'm mistaken, the two of you were being blackmailed."

They glanced at each other, and then at me.

"I don't know what you mean," Boris said.

"There's no point in denying it. I know what happened. Arthur Longstaff told you that unless you voted to renew the contract for Tip Top Construction, you'd never see your dogs alive again. And you daren't tell anyone, for fear of what he might do to the dogs."

"You're right," Maisy said. "But when I first contacted you, I didn't know what had happened to Toto. Longstaff didn't contact me until the next day."

"Likewise," Boris said. "When you came to see me, I had no idea that Longstaff had Hector."

"This isn't the first time he's done this. You two weren't

on the council four years ago, were you?"

They shook their heads.

"A similar thing happened back then. He managed to sway the vote by blackmailing a number of dog owners."

"That's despicable!" Boris said. "The man should be sent to prison."

"Don't worry, he will be. But for something a lot more serious than kidnapping dogs."

Chapter 14

I called at the front desk of Washbridge police station, and waited in line behind a man who was complaining about his neighbour's music. Not that it was too loud, but that he was playing jazz. The desk sergeant dismissed his complaint—unfairly in my opinion.

When it was my turn, the desk sergeant made a call, and said that Detective Riley would be with me shortly. It turned out that his idea of 'shortly' and mine, were some distance apart. An hour later, when Leo Riley finally showed his face, he didn't apologise for keeping me waiting, and he certainly didn't look very pleased to see me. I was pretty sure the man *could* smile, but he had yet to prove it.

"Come with me," he snapped.

I followed him into a small interview room just off the reception area. He didn't sit down, and he didn't offer me a chair. We just stood there facing one another.

"What do you want?" he said.

"How do you always manage to be so charming?"

"I don't have time to be charming, I'm busy. What do you want?"

"I've tracked down three lost dogs."

"Lost dogs? I'm glad to see that you found your *leash*." He laughed at his own joke. No one else was going to.

"I have important information. Do you want it or not?"

"About lost dogs? They're not really very high on my priority list."

"No. It's a much more serious matter."

"Go on then. Hurry up, I don't have all day."

"Arthur Longstaff is the CEO of Tip Top Construction.

He's been blackmailing council members so they'll award his company construction contracts. He did the same thing four years ago."

"And of course, you have proof of this?"

"The council members in question will testify to that effect. I can give you their names and addresses, if you like?"

"Okay, but you didn't need to see me for that. You could have told the desk sergeant."

"There's something else. And, this should interest you."

"What now?"

"You have an unsolved murder case on your books from four years ago. A Joseph Lewis."

"What about it?" Riley suddenly seemed a lot more interested.

"Arthur Longstaff murdered Lewis."

"What proof do you have?"

"Longstaff recently arranged for dogs belonging to two councillors to be kidnapped. He threatened to kill them unless the councillors voted to award a contract to his company. He did the same thing four years ago. Back then, most of the councillors took the easy way out, and voted for Tip Top Construction, after which their dogs were returned to them. Joseph Lewis wasn't easily intimidated. He confronted Arthur Longstaff at his country house, and probably threatened to go to the police."

"You know this how?"

"Because his dog told me."

"What?"

"Just joking. When Lewis's body was found, he was covered in dog hairs from several different breeds. Some of the hair was from his own dog. The one that had been kidnapped."

"It's hardly surprising that he had his own dog's hairs on his jumper."

"Except that the jumper he was wearing had been a birthday present from his wife. She'd knitted it herself, and had only given it to him on the morning of his murder—*after* the dog was kidnapped. That means Lewis must have found his dog at Longstaff's house."

"Why didn't we know about the jumper?"

"That's a very good question. My guess is no one thought to ask Patricia Lewis, and she was too upset at the time to think about birthday presents or jumpers."

"That's all very interesting, but it only proves that Lewis found his dog. Where's the connection to Longstaff?"

"If you get someone up to Longstaff's place quickly, and search his kennels, you'll find Lewis' dog is still there. But you'd better be quick. Once Longstaff realises the other dogs are gone, he'll know the game is up, and make a run for it."

"What other dogs?"

"The ones belonging to the council members who were being blackmailed. I've reunited them with their owners."

"None of this is going to get me a murder conviction."

"Maybe not, but you have the DNA of the murderer on file. You now have probable cause. If you test Longstaff's DNA, my guess is, you'll find a match."

Riley hesitated for a moment. "I'll have someone go over there now to check it out."

"There's no need to thank me."

He showed me the door without another word.

***

Jack had bought the snow globe from a man outside West Chipping railway station, so I decided to drive over there to see if he was still plying his trade. I parked close to the police station. It was the first time I'd actually seen Jack's new place of work. I considered popping in to say hello, but decided Jack might not appreciate me turning up out of the blue.

I made my way on foot to the railway station, which was only a five-minute walk away. As I turned the corner, I could see that the man had set up his makeshift stall at the side of the building. After a quick phone call to Daze, I cast a spell which would block my sup-identity from the wizard. If he realised that I was a witch, he would know I was onto him, and be gone before Daze arrived.

I was rather proud of the 'block' spell, which I'd only recently concocted. If it worked as designed, it should ensure he would see me as a human.

"They're very pretty," I said.

"Best snow globes in West Chipping." He treated me to a gap-toothed grin. "Look at the detail." He held one up. "You can even see the furniture inside the rooms. Every detail is perfect."

"How much are you asking for these?"

"Forty pounds."

"That's expensive."

"You won't find better anywhere else."

"I've seen real houses that look very similar to these."

He shrugged. "Do you want to buy one or not?"

"In fact, I've seen houses which were identical to these.

Now, where was it I saw them? Oh yes, I remember. In Candlefield."

He looked shocked. "How do you know about Candlefield?"

"I'm a witch."

"You're not a witch. I'd be able to tell."

"Right, buddy." The voice came from behind him. He turned around to find Daze standing there, with Blaze by her side. "Time you took a trip back to Candlefield."

"No, please! It's all a mistake. I didn't shrink them. That was someone else. I'm just selling them for him."

"Tell it to the authorities."

Daze quickly threw the wire mesh net over him, and he disappeared in a puff of smoke.

"What shall we do about these houses?" I asked Daze.

"Blaze and I will take the snow globes back with us. I'm sure we'll be able to find another wizard who can reverse the spells, and put the houses back in their rightful place."

"I've got one of these globes back at the house. Jack bought it for me."

"That's a bit unfortunate."

"I can't keep it. I don't want to deprive someone of their home. I'll magic it back over to you in Candlefield."

"What will you tell Jack?"

"I'll think of something."

***

"What are you doing, Jill?" Jules looked up at me. I was standing on a chair.

"I'm trying to get this stupid cuckoo out of the clock."

"Why?"

"I told Mrs V that the cuckoo from the clock in my office has gone away for repair. In fact, it broke into smithereens, and was thrown out with the trash. I've got to find an identical cuckoo, like the one in this clock, so I can put it back in mine before she realises."

"Where will you get it from?"

"I've no idea. Normally, I'd ask Armi because he's a member of the Cuckoo Clock Appreciation Society, but he'd probably tell Mrs V."

I eventually managed to get the bird out of the 'good' clock, and then consulted the Yellow Pages. I wasn't sure what to look for: clocks, clock repairs? But then I noticed a section for cuckoo clocks; there was a single entry under it. The shop was called Cuckoos Unlimited, and according to the advert, it kept the most extensive stock of cuckoo clock parts in the UK. Luckily for me it was right here in Washbridge, located in a back street on the other side of town.

"I'm going to take a walk over there, Jules."

"Okay. Good luck."

I was going to need it.

En route, I called in at Coffee Triangle. It was drum day, so I ordered my coffee 'to go.' When I arrived at Cuckoos Unlimited, I wasn't sure if it was open. The blinds were down, so I couldn't even see through the window. But when I tried the door, it opened and a bell rang. From somewhere behind the counter, an old man with long, thinning, grey hair appeared. He had a runny nose.

"Yes, young lady, what can I do for you?"

"I'm trying to find a cuckoo like this one." I took the bird out of my bag.

"Ah yes. This is the Tweetling3617."

"Do you have one?"

"I think so, yes." He started to rummage around. The small shop was packed with all manner of parts. There seemed to be no organisation; it was just one big mess. And yet, he seemed to know what he was doing.

"It should be over in that far corner. Wait here while I take a look."

A few minutes later, he came back holding an identical bird.

"There you are, the Tweetling3617. Not many of these about now. It was replaced a few years ago by the Tweetling3618."

"That's great. How much is it?"

"Let me check." He took out a dusty catalogue. "The Tweetling3615, the 3616—here it is—the 3617. That's thirty-one pounds and seventy-five pence, please."

On my way back to the office, I noticed the shop which the twins had hoped to rent, was now being renovated. There were workmen inside, and a new sign had been erected. It had white letters on a blue background, and simply read *'She Sells.'* How very curious. She sells what?

Kathy was behind the counter in Ever. She wasn't serving anyone, so I popped inside.

"I see they've let the shop across the road?"

"Yeah, a couple of days ago. Things seem to be moving pretty fast—they put the sign up yesterday."

"So I see. 'She Sells'? What's that all about?"

"Beats me."

"I hope it's not wool."

"Yeah, me too. Or we'll never hear the end of it."

When I got back to my building, I could barely get in the door. There was a queue of young women stretching all the way upstairs.

"Excuse me, please," I said.

"Hey, get in line!" A young woman with a nose piercing, shouted at me. "There's a queue here. Can't you see it?"

"Yes, but I'm—"

"If you're here for the interview, get in line like the rest of us."

"What interview?"

"For I-Sweat of course. They're recruiting instructors."

"I'm not here to interview for I-Sweat. I have the office at the top of the stairs."

"Oh. Sorry, love. I thought you were a bit out of shape to be an instructor."

Cheeky madam!

Chapter 15

It had taken me most of the afternoon, but I'd finally managed to get both of the stupid cuckoo birds back into the stupid clocks.

"Why did you do that?" Winky said.

"I've mended the clock."

"I know *what* you've done. I asked *why* you've done it. It's been nice and peaceful in here without that stupid bird cuckooing every hour."

"The clocks were a gift from Armi. It's only right that we should keep them in good repair."

"And what about during the night, when I'm trying to sleep? *You're* not the one who has to put up with it. I bet you don't have a cuckoo clock in your bedroom."

"Well, no."

"Exactly. But you expect me to sleep in here with that awful row. Don't blame me if you find it smashed to pieces in the morning."

"And who exactly would I blame?"

I was feeling drained after my cuckoo exploits, so I treated myself to an early finish. When I arrived home, I couldn't get my car onto the drive because there was something blocking the pavement. It looked like some kind of temporary bus stop. Then I heard a small engine. I turned around to find Mr Hosey coming down the street on his silly little train. He tooted the horn a couple of times by way of a greeting before pulling up next to me. There was no one in either of the carriages.

"Hello there, Jill."

"Mr Hosey. Is this yours?" I pointed to the object which

was blocking my driveway.
"That's one of the train-stops."
"Train-stops?"
"I have four of them on the circuit in case anyone wants to get on board."
"You don't seem to have *any* passengers at all at the moment."
"It will probably pick up later."
"You've put the train-stop smack bang in the middle of the entrance to my driveway, I can't get the car on the drive."
"I'll move it as soon as I've finished with the train for the day."
"How long is that likely to be?"
"Another hour or so."
"What am I supposed to do with my car in the meantime?"
"Can't you leave it on the road? An hour will fly by."
"Couldn't you just move the train-stop a few metres down the pavement, so it isn't blocking my drive?"
"If I did that, Jill, the four stops wouldn't be equidistant from each other."
"Does that really matter?"
"Of course. If someone pays to go on the train, they'll expect to get the correct yardage."
"You charge people to go on *this* thing?"
"Not exactly. I'm not allowed to levy a charge as such, but I do ask for voluntary donations."
"Oh?"
"Of five pounds."
"So the voluntary donation has a fixed amount?"
"Not as such. Five pounds is the *minimum* suggested

donation. People are free to donate more, obviously."

"I see. Well, I'm sorry, Mr Hosey, but I need to get my car onto the drive, so I'm afraid you're going to have to move the train-stop."

"I'm not sure how I'll explain this to my customers when they realise they've been given short measure."

"I'm pretty sure no one will notice."

Still grumbling to himself, he moved the train-stop beyond the end of the driveway.

"Thank you."

Jack arrived home just after six.

"I think I may have upset one of our neighbours."

"Which one this time? Megan?"

"No."

"Not Mrs Rollo?"

"Mr Hosey. He'd put his train-stop in front of our drive."

"His what?"

"Train-stop. He has four of them along the route. It was blocking the drive."

"Is he crazy? Why didn't he put it a few metres further down?"

"He likes them to be equidistant from each other. Otherwise people might complain that they'd been given short measure. Hold on! Why am I even trying to explain this? The man is making me as crazy as he is."

Jack was staring at the mantelpiece. "Where's the globe?"

Oh, bum!

"I—err—I told you. I thought Kathy might like one."

"Weren't you going to buy one for her today?"

"I decided to show her mine first. Just to make sure she likes it."

"Why did you have to leave it with her? Couldn't she make up her mind there and then?"

"She wasn't in when I took it around. I left it with Peter, and asked him to show it to her."

"Oh, okay."

What was I supposed to do now? I'd sent the globe back to Candlefield so the house could be restored to its rightful owner, but I could hardly tell Jack that. Where was I going to find a replacement?

***

First thing the next morning, I magicked myself over to Candlefield. Aunt Lucy had arranged for me to meet with Desmond Cloverleaf, the husband of Gloria who had died in the supermarket after becoming hysterical with laughter. Desmond cut a sorrowful figure; he was obviously still grief-stricken.

"You must be Jill," he said.

"Yes. Aunt Lucy said it would be okay to come and talk to you."

"Do come in. Can I get you a drink or anything?"

"No, please don't trouble yourself, Mr Cloverleaf. Let's just sit down and talk."

"Okay."

In the living room, there were photos of Mr Cloverleaf and his wife everywhere. He glanced at each one of them before taking a seat.

"I realise this is difficult for you, Mr Cloverleaf, but I'd like to try to establish exactly what happened to your wife."

"I understand, but it's still very raw as you can imagine."

"Of course. Has the hospital told you the cause of your wife's death?"

"They said her heart gave way. It was the strain of the laughter. I assume you heard about that."

"Yes, Aunt Lucy told me. In fact, I actually witnessed someone else die in the same way."

"Really?" He seemed surprised.

"Yes. There's been more than one incident."

"I wasn't aware of that. Maybe someone did tell me, but I haven't really been with it. The doctor said Gloria had laughed so hard, and for so long, that her heart couldn't stand the strain."

"Were you with her at the time?"

"No, she was doing the weekly shop. She liked to do it alone; she said I slowed her down."

"Is there anything you can think of that could have sparked off the laughter?"

"Nothing. She was in the confectionery aisle at the time. There's nothing particularly funny there. And besides, Gloria was never really one for laughing out loud. She would normally just smile or give the occasional chuckle. For instance, the night before she died we'd been to Candlefield Social to see Kenny Pope. Have you heard of him?"

"I don't think so."

"He's a comedian. He was very funny. Everyone was in hysterics except for Gloria; she barely cracked a smile. So why would she be laughing in the confectionery aisle of the supermarket? It doesn't make any sense. Do you think

you'll be able to get to the bottom of it?"
"I'm certainly going to try, Mr Cloverleaf."

Desmond Cloverleaf and I talked for some time. Afterwards, I made my way over to Cuppy C. I was ready to kill for a blueberry muffin and a cup of tea. When I got there, Laura was working in the cake shop, and to my surprise Flora was behind the counter in the tea room.

"Hello, Jill." Flora greeted me with what appeared to be a genuine smile.

"I thought you worked in the flower shop in the marketplace?"

"I did, but I got talking to the twins, and they told me they could still do with another pair of hands, so I asked them if I could have a job here. They agreed because I'd had experience working in a shop already, so I gave in my notice and here I am. It makes a pleasant change from selling flowers."

"I'm sure it does."

"What can I get you, Jill?"

"A blueberry muffin and a cup of tea, please."

"I believe you get the staff discount?"

"That's right. Seventy percent."

What? No harm in trying.

Flora seemed very comfortable behind the counter, and had served me in next to no time. She was wise to my ploy though, and only gave me twenty percent discount. Drat!

Something about Flora and Laura had been bothering me ever since I'd seen them with Miles and Mindy. I was even more concerned now they were both working in Cuppy C. And where were the twins? Out shopping probably. I hoped they knew what they were doing setting on these two ice maidens.

***

My phone rang. It was Patricia Lewis.

"Jill? I wanted to thank you for getting Desi back. I never thought I'd see him again."

"My pleasure. I guess he was pleased to see you."

"He's never left my side since he came home." Her voice faltered. "It's the next best thing to having Joseph back."

"Have the police said anything about the murder case?"

"Not much. A new detective came to see me. I didn't like him very much."

"Was his name Riley?"

"That's him. When I asked him what was happening, he said they were working on a new lead, but wouldn't say any more. Anyway, thanks again."

It was time to get to work on the Jessica Lambert case. She'd come to see me because her boyfriend, Paul, was no longer acting like her boyfriend. She insisted he'd become a different person, and had started going out by himself when they would normally stay in together.

I waited outside his flat until he came out, and then followed him on foot into the centre of Washbridge. He went to a bar that I hadn't come across before. It was called Bar Scarlet. After he'd gone inside, I gave it a few minutes, and then followed him.

I was surprised to find that the majority of people in the bar were vampires. I was used to coming across sups in

Washbridge, but it was usually just one or two of them at a time. I'd never seen so many sups in one place. The humans were outnumbered twenty to one. The music was loud, but not unpleasant, and the atmosphere seemed very relaxed. The bar was doing a roaring trade. Paul made his way towards the far side of the room, but by the time I'd eventually fought my way through the crowd, there was no sign of him.

"Excuse me?" I approached a young, male vampire who was standing by himself. "I'm looking for a friend of mine—a human. Have you seen him?"

"No, sorry. I haven't seen any humans tonight."

I asked several other vampires, but none of them had seen Paul—or at least so they said. After a couple more circuits of the bar, there was still no sign of him. He must have somehow doubled back, and left without me noticing.

Well done, Jill! All you had to do was keep tabs on him. My adoptive father would not have been impressed.

Chapter 16

I'd arranged to meet with Douglas Beauford. It was his wife, Mabel, who had died in Holo while I was in there with Aunt Lucy. When I'd phoned ahead, he'd readily agreed to see me. Unlike Desmond Cloverleaf, Douglas Beauford wasn't exactly the grieving widower. He greeted me with a huge smile.

"Douglas Beauford?" I wasn't sure I had the right house.

"Yep. That's me." He was a wizard with the fakest of tans. "You wanted to talk to me about Mabel?"

"Yes, please."

"Come in then. Watch the cats; they're everywhere." I glanced around, but didn't see a single cat. "Mabel could never resist a cat. She'd take in any old stray, but they'll soon be gone."

"If you don't mind me saying so, Mr Beauford, you don't seem awfully upset about your wife's passing."

"Upset about Mabel? Nah. Me and Mabel were over years ago. We still shared the same house, but that's about it. I have my life. She had hers."

"I assume you heard how she died."

"I did, and to tell you the truth, I thought it was a bit weird. You could say many things about Mabel, but you would never describe her as someone who laughed a lot. She'd barely cracked a smile in the last five years. She didn't even laugh at my jokes, and everybody laughs at my jokes. Do you want to hear one?"

"No thanks, not right now. Had she been ill or complained of any health problems?"

"Nah. Not to me, anyway. We didn't talk much. We

said 'morning,' but that was about it. She still made all my meals though, but only because I gave her money every month."

"What about the day before she died?"

"I didn't see her. She went out with a friend, Elizabeth Tagg, the night before she died. They were always out together. Either to bingo or dancing. It might be worth you talking to Elizabeth."

"Do you happen to have her contact details?"

"There's an address book next to the phone."

It was obvious that Douglas neither knew nor cared what had happened to his wife—all rather sad, I thought.

I made a note of Elizabeth Tagg's phone number, and then left.

I could hear Aunt Lucy and Lester arguing before I even walked in the door. As soon as they heard me, they stopped. Lester was sitting at the kitchen table. Aunt Lucy was standing next to him; she was rather red in the face.

"Sorry if I interrupted," I said. "I can leave, if you want me to?"

"It's all right. Come in, Jill. I wanted to see you, anyway."

"Are you sure?"

"Yes, come in. You'll never guess what Lester is thinking of doing."

"I'm right here, Lucy," he said. "In case you hadn't noticed."

"He's going to apply for a job as a Grim Reaper."

Wow! I hadn't seen that coming.

"I didn't realise it was possible to apply to be a Grim Reaper. I assumed it was something you were born into."

"That's what I thought too," Lester said. "But it seems there are two types of reaper. There are those who are born into it—they're a bit of a strange breed—neither human nor sup."

Strange was the right word. I remembered my date with Jim Keeper the Grim Reaper.

Lester continued. "The other reapers are those trained to do the job. It's a twelve-month training course to qualify. It's good pay, even while you're training."

"I'm not surprised that it's good pay," Aunt Lucy interrupted. "Nobody in their right mind would want to do that miserable job."

"Beggars can't be choosers, Lucy, I've told you. I've been applying for other jobs, but so far I haven't even been able to get an interview anywhere else. At least these people are prepared to see me."

"I bet they are. They'll probably interview anybody who's stupid enough to contact them."

"I'm not standing for this, Lucy. There's no talking to you when you're in this mood." Lester stood up and stormed out.

"I think you're being a bit hard on him, Aunt Lucy. He's only trying to get a job."

"I know he is. But it's the thought of being married to a Grim Reaper; it gives me the creeps. Every time he came home from work, I'd be wondering who he'd dispatched that day. Anyway, let's forget about that. With a bit of luck, he won't get the job."

"Aunt Lucy! That's a bit harsh!"

"Sorry. Don't tell him I said that. Are you making any progress with Gloria?"

"Nothing so far. I've spoken to Desmond. He's really

cut up as you can imagine, but he couldn't throw much light on it. He did say that Gloria didn't laugh a lot."

"He's right. Some people will laugh out loud at anything, but Gloria would just smile, which makes this all the more strange."

"I've also been to see the husband of the woman who died while we were in Holo."

"How's he holding up?"

"He's fine; he doesn't seem to care. They had a strange relationship. They shared the same house, but other than that, they lived totally separate lives, and barely saw one another. I'm going to talk to a friend of hers to see if she can tell me anything. By the way, where is Candlefield Social?"

"You surely don't want to go there, do you?"

"Why? What's wrong with it?"

"It's a bit run down. There are much nicer places in Candlefield. I can give you the names of a few clubs you'd enjoy much more."

"It's not for a night out. It seems that Gloria was there the night before she died."

"Gloria went to Candlefield Social? I am surprised. I wouldn't have thought it was her kind of thing."

"According to Desmond, they were there together. It's a long shot, but I thought I might call in and take a look."

"You know where the hospital is, don't you?"

"Yes."

"Candlefield Social is on the next street down from there. You walk past the hospital, and keep on going until you come to Tadpole Avenue."

"Tadpole?"

"It backs onto Frog Close."

"Okay, thanks. And, Aunt Lucy—take it easy on Lester."

"I will. Don't worry."

I was just about to leave when the twins turned up. They were beaming.

"I'm glad we've caught you two together," Amber said. "We've got big news."

"Really big news." Pearl nodded.

Whenever the twins had news, it was usually some kind of half-baked scheme. The fact that this was *big* news had me really worried.

"What kind of news?" Aunt Lucy looked as apprehensive as I felt.

"It's about our housewarming parties," Pearl said.

"Have you reached a compromise?" I asked.

"We have." Amber sounded very pleased with herself. "We've decided we're both going to have our housewarming party this Sunday."

"Both of you? But don't you remember I said you'll be inviting the same people to both parties? They can't be in two places at the same time."

"We've come up with a brilliant plan," Pearl said. "Haven't we, Amber?"

Amber nodded. "We have. Would you like to hear it?"

Probably not. I'd heard so-called brilliant plans from the twins before.

"Go on," Aunt Lucy said. "Spit it out. I know you're dying to tell us."

"We've decided we'll both have a housewarming party starting at four-thirty on Sunday. We're going to write down the names of all the people who we want to invite, and put them into a hat."

Aunt Lucy and I exchanged a despairing glance.

Pearl continued. "We'll draw out the names one at a time. The first name that comes out will go to Amber's housewarming at four-thirty. The next name that comes out will go to mine at four-thirty. We'll carry on doing that until we've taken all the names out of the hat."

"Hang on. Let me see if I understand this," I said. "Half the people are going to your housewarming, and the other half are going to Amber's?"

"To start with, yes, but then comes the ingenious part."

Please, spare me from the ingenious part.

"At seven-thirty, a bus will arrive and take all the people who have been at my housewarming to Amber's, and then pick up all the people who have been at Amber's, and bring them back to mine. That way, everybody will have been to both parties. Didn't I tell you it was ingenious? What do you think?"

"I don't have words." I sighed.

"I do," Aunt Lucy said. "It's a stupid idea."

"No it's not, Mother." Pearl sounded indignant. "It's a brilliant idea. This way we both get to have our party on the same day."

"Yes, but you're asking people to go to one party, and then get on a bus to go to the other party."

"What's wrong with that?" Amber said.

"I can't wait to hear you explain this to Grandma."

Aunt Lucy and I both laughed. The twins were not amused.

***

Jack and I arrived home at more or less the same time. It

was his turn to cook. Yay! But, before he could start, there was a knock at the door. If it was Mr Hosey, I was going to tell him where he could shove his train-stop. It turned out to be Kathy.

"Hi. I hope you don't mind me calling around unannounced, but Pete's taken Lizzie and Mikey to Tom Tom."

"Lizzie too?"

"They're entering a talent contest together. Mikey on drums, and Lizzie singing."

Boy, oh boy.

"They want to get some practice together. It was Pete's turn to take them, so I thought I'd pop over here and say hello to my favourite sister."

"You'd better come in. Jack! It's Kathy."

"Hi, Kathy. This is a nice surprise. You didn't need to make a special journey just to bring the snow globe back."

"Sorry?" Kathy looked understandably puzzled.

"The snow globe. It would've done anytime."

"What snow globe is that, Jack?"

"The one that Jill left for you to look at."

They both stared at me.

"Err—Yeah. I left it with Peter. Didn't he tell you?"

"He never mentioned anything to me about a snow globe. What about it?"

"Jack bought me a lovely snow globe. Didn't you, Jack?"

"I did, yeah. Although I've almost forgotten what it looks like."

I ignored his jibe. "I thought you might like one too."

"I see." She obviously didn't, and who could blame her?

"I took it around to your house, but you weren't in, so I

left it with Peter for you to look at."

"He must have forgotten."

"That must be it. Anyway, let's have a coffee."

After we'd finished our drinks, Jack went upstairs to get changed. As soon as he was out of earshot, Kathy grabbed me. "What's all this about a snow globe? I've seen Pete. He would have said something."

"Shush! I dropped it and it smashed."

"You clumsy —"

"Don't let Jack hear you. I told him I took it to your place, so I'd have time to find an identical one. Just play along, will you?"

"I'm not lying to him, Jill."

"You don't have to lie. Just don't tell him the truth."

"When will you ever learn? Why don't you come clean? You do the same thing every single time. You dig yourself into a deeper and deeper hole."

"I know what I'm doing, Kathy."

Just then, there was another knock at the door. Kathy followed me through to the hallway. I opened the door to find Megan Lovemore standing there.

"Hello, Megan," I said.

"Hi, Jill. Actually, it isn't you I came to see."

"Are you after Jack?"

"No. I was hoping to speak to your sister. I saw her pull onto your driveway."

Kathy stepped forward.

"Hi, again, Kathy." Megan beamed.

"Hello," Kathy said, stony-faced.

"I've got a bit of a problem, Kathy. I've got a mole."

"So what?" Kathy pushed up her sleeve. "I have lots of them."

"Not that kind of mole. The kind that digs up your back garden."

"Oh, right," Kathy said. "Of course."

"I'm after some advice on how to deal with it. I wondered if you'd ask Peter to come over to see if he can sort me out."

"Sort you out?"

"I'd pay him, obviously."

Chapter 17

Mrs V was at her desk when I arrived at work the next morning.

"Morning, Mrs V."

"Morning, Jill. I'm pleased to see you've got the cuckoo clock in your office repaired."

"Oh yes, piece of cake. Nothing to it."

"I told Armi that—"

Just then the phone on her desk rang. "Hello? Pardon? What did you say? I'm sorry? No, I certainly would not. No, I'm not interested. No. Goodbye."

"What was that all about, Mrs V?"

"I don't know. Some young man. He said he thought I was very pretty, and asked if I'd like to go out on a date with him. The cheek of some people. What's got into youngsters these days?"

"Did he mention his name?"

"Yes, I think so, but I can't remember what he said."

"Was it Jethro, by any chance?"

"That was it. Cheeky young man!"

Oh dear. Jethro had obviously called to ask Jules out. I hadn't thought to tell Peter that Jules was actually job sharing, and wasn't in every day.

"What am I going to do?" Winky said, as soon as I walked through the door.

"Do about what?"

"It's terrible! It's just terrible."

"I know that cuckoo clock can be annoying, but it's only once an hour."

"Not the clock. I don't care about the stupid clock."

"What's wrong then?"

"It's Bella."

"What's happened now? Don't tell me Bonnie and Clive have changed their minds and taken her with them?"

"No. They've already left. Bella is with Mrs Shuman now."

"Socks isn't chasing her again, is he?"

"Stop going on about my brother. That was a one-off mistake. He won't do that again."

"You're more trusting than I am. What's the problem then?"

"You said I'd still be able to see her when she moved to her new apartment."

"Can't you?"

"No, her new apartment is on the side of the building. We can't use semaphore because we're not in line of sight of each other. I can't even use the helicopter because I'm flying blind once it goes around the corner of the building. How on earth are we going to keep in touch?"

"Can't she use her phone?"

"She doesn't have access to one now. She used to use Bonnie's, but she's taken it with her. We need to come up with something, and quick."

"We?"

"Yes, we."

"I'm not sure why I'm involved?"

"Because you were the one who put her into an apartment where I can't see her."

"Hang on a minute. I thought you said I was the best thing since sliced bread when I found her a new home?"

"Are you going to help or not?"

"Okay, leave it with me. I'll give it some thought." It

was time to take his mind off Bella. "I haven't seen you working on the time machine for a while. How's it going?"

"It's hard to focus while I'm worrying about Bella, but it's almost finished. I'm on the final trials now. It'll soon be ready."

"I look forward to that, and to collecting my winnings."

***

Jessica Lambeth had made an appointment to see me at ten o'clock. By ten-thirty there was still no sign of her. How very strange! She'd been so keen for me to find out what was going on with her boyfriend. Why would she miss our meeting? I thought I'd better give her a call to make sure everything was okay. I rang the number that she'd given me, but there was no answer. I could have left it at that, but I had a nagging feeling that something was wrong. I had her address, so I decided to go around there—just in case.

Jessica's apartment was not far from where I used to live before I moved in with Jack. I knocked on her door; there was no answer. I tried again, louder this time. It was Paul who eventually answered the door. He was staring straight at me, but his eyes were dead.

"Yes?" he sounded like a robot.

"I'm here to see Jessica."

"Why do you want to see her?"

"She's a friend of mine."

"What's your name?"

"Jill Gooder."

"Wait there." He pushed the door to, and went back

inside. Moments later, he reappeared. "She says she's fine, and that she doesn't want to see you."

That simply didn't ring true. Jessica had been adamant there was something wrong with her boyfriend, and desperate for me to find out what. Now, suddenly she'd lost all interest, and wouldn't even speak to me? Something wasn't right. Maybe he was keeping her there against her will. Maybe she was hurt.

"I need to see her." I stepped forward.

"You can't." He held the door, but he was no match for me after I'd cast the 'power' spell. I found Jessica sitting on the sofa in the lounge.

"Jessica?" I pushed the door shut so we'd be alone.

There was something very different about her. Something very wrong. She had the same dead look in her eyes that Paul had.

"Hello, Jill." She too sounded like a robot.

"Jessica, you were meant to come to my office this morning?"

"I forgot, sorry."

"Don't you want to pursue the case?"

"No, everything's okay now. I made a mistake. There's no need for you to do any more. Thank you for your help."

"But Jessica, I think you could be right about Paul."

"Everything is fine. Please let me have your bill. Thank you. Goodbye."

This was not the same woman who'd sat opposite me only a few days earlier. She looked as though she'd been drugged, and was completely out of it. Had Paul done this to her?

Something was going on, and I was determined to find out what it was.

***

I magicked myself to Candlefield, and then made my way to Tadpole Road. It was a narrow road with unremarkable houses on either side. Halfway along it, I came across Candlefield Social. The sign had obviously once read 'Candlefield Social Club,' but the word 'club' had dropped off, leaving only the imprint of where the letters had once been. Everyone now referred to it simply as Candlefield Social.

On one of the boards next to the entrance was a list of all upcoming acts. There were two comedians, a number of solo singers, a ventriloquist, and a magician.

A magician in Candlefield? Someone was having a laugh.

I tried the front door; it was open.

There was no one in the foyer, so I went through to what was obviously the main hall. The lights were dimmed. A single spotlight was trained on the man on stage. He was obviously practising his act, so I stopped and listened to a few of his jokes. He simply wasn't funny. The jokes were, at best, cringeworthy.

He was still going through his routine as I made my way to the far side of the auditorium where there was a door marked *'Manager – Private.'* When I knocked, someone shouted *'Come in.'* Inside, was a man smoking a pipe. The smell coming from it wasn't tobacco. What was it? Raspberry? Blueberry?

"It's strawberry." He must have noticed me sniffing the

air. "Do you like it?"

I did. It was surprisingly pleasant. "It's very unusual."

"How can I help you?"

"Are you the manager?"

"Yes, I'm Terry Roth." When he walked around the desk, I noticed he had a slight limp.

"My name is Jill Gooder. I'm a private investigator."

"I've heard of you. You're that level seven witch, aren't you?"

"Not exactly. I was offered the chance to move to level seven."

"That's right. I remember now. What brings you here?"

"I wanted to talk to you about a woman who died recently. She'd been in this club the night before. You might have seen something in the paper about it. She was laughing uncontrollably, and then collapsed and died."

"Oh yes, I do remember that. I seem to remember the headline in The Candle was: *'Died Laughing.'* Very insensitive, I thought. So, how can I help you?"

"I wondered if you'd had reports of anyone being taken ill on the night she was here?"

"We haven't had anyone take ill in the club for several weeks now. Certainly not while Kenny has been performing. He always has them in hysterics."

"Is that the guy who's out there now?"

"Yes. He likes to rehearse his full routine beforehand."

"Look, I don't mean to be rude, but I was just listening to him, and I didn't think he was at all funny."

"To tell you the truth, neither do I. His jokes are terrible, but every time he appears here, he has the audience in hysterics."

"With that routine? How?"

"It's a mystery to me too. We gave him a try out a few years ago, and he went down like a lead balloon, so I had to drop him. After that, he disappeared off the scene for a few years. Perhaps he was reworking his act; I don't know. But whatever he did seems to have worked because since he re-emerged, he's been going down a storm with audiences."

***

There was no sign of Jack when I got home. That wasn't particularly unusual; he could turn up at any hour. I got changed, and was wondering what to cook for dinner when there was a knock at the door. It was a tall man with striking red hair and a red beard.

"Jill, thank goodness you're in."

"Sorry, do I know you?"

"I was hoping you'd be in. I need to speak to you before they catch up with me."

Just then my phone rang. I'd left it on the kitchen worktop. "Just a second." I pushed the door closed.

It was Jack on the phone. "Jill, you'll never guess what."

"You've got to work late?"

"Got it in one. It's probably going to be eleven o'clock at the earliest. You'd better get yourself some dinner; I'll grab something on the job."

"Okay. I'll see you later."

I hurried back to the door. I wanted to find out who the man was. I'd never seen him before, and yet he'd spoken to me as though we were long lost friends.

There was no one there, so I stepped outside and looked down the street, but there was no sign of him. Maybe he'd gone around the back of the house. I put on some shoes and went to check. There was no one there either. Could he have slipped into the house while I was talking to Jack? It was possible because I hadn't locked the door. I hurried back inside.

"Hello? I've got a baseball bat, and I'm not afraid to use it."

I checked downstairs. He was nowhere to be seen. I made my way slowly up the stairs. I tried our bedroom—nothing. Then the bathroom—nothing. And finally, the spare bedroom—I could barely get in it myself. He was nowhere to be seen.

Where had he gone, and who was he?

Chapter 18

The next morning, I arrived at the office before Jules. When she turned up, the first thing she did was bring me a cup of tea.

"Be careful with that, Jules."

She was only carrying the one cup, but tea was still slopping into the saucer.

"Sorry, Jill. I just can't seem to carry cups."

"Maybe, in future, it would be better if you give me a shout when the tea is ready, and I can come and get it."

"That's a good idea." As she put the cup down onto my desk, more tea slopped over the side. "Sorry, Jill."

"It's okay."

"What about sugar? I didn't put any in, because I don't really understand how much you take."

"It's okay. I've got some in my drawer. I'll see to it."

She turned around, and was about to leave.

"Jules. Just a second. I thought you should know that Mrs V took a call from Jethro, yesterday."

"Why was he calling Mrs V?"

"He didn't intend to. Peter gave him the office number so he could get in touch with you, but he omitted to tell him that you don't work here every day. He just happened to ring when Mrs V was in."

"What did she say to him?"

"That's just it. I think Jethro must have been nervous. He heard a female voice, assumed it was you, and asked Mrs V out."

"Oh heck! What did she say?"

"She more or less told him to get lost."

"Wait a minute. Does that mean Jethro thinks it was me

who told him to get lost?"

"It's possible, yeah."

"I knew I should have called him. All that 'playing hard to get' didn't really work out, did it?"

"Sorry about that, Jules."

"He probably won't want to hear from me now."

"I'm sure he will—if you explain what happened."

"Have you got his number, Jill?"

"Yeah. I checked the call log after Mrs V had spoken to him." I passed Jules the slip of paper I'd scribbled the number on.

Winky had been remarkably quiet since I'd arrived. It was almost ten-thirty when he eventually crawled out from under the sofa. He stretched, and gave a big yawn.

"Nice of you to join us," I said.

"You'd sleep in too if you'd been woken up every hour by a stupid cuckoo clock."

I chuckled at the thought.

"I don't know what you're laughing at. It's not funny. I need my rest. How am I meant to be at my best if I'm woken up every hour?"

"Why don't you put those earmuffs on?"

"For the hundredth time, they're not earmuffs. They're ear defenders."

He jumped onto the sofa, and from somewhere, produced a tablet.

"Where did you get that from?"

"I have my sources. If I'd waited for you to come up with a solution to my communication problems, I would have been waiting forever. Bella and I have decided to communicate via Skype."

"Has Bella got a tablet?"

"It turns out that the old lady she lives with has one; her son bought it for her. She doesn't have a clue what to do with it—she's been using it as a placemat. So now, Bella has acquired it."

The distinctive Skype call sound caught his attention.

"Hiya, Sweetie," he said, to the screen.

"Hello, lover." I heard a voice call back.

Was I going to have to listen to these two all morning?

"Say hello to Bella." Winky held the tablet towards me.

"Hello, Bella," I shouted.

She purred regally.

"Hey, Winky," I whispered.

He put the tablet to one side. "What?"

"Have you told Bella about your time machine?"

"Shush! She'll worry if she knows I'm going to be time travelling."

"Okay. Mum's the word."

***

I'd made no real progress with Gloria Cloverleaf's sudden and mysterious death. Her husband had tried to be helpful, but was obviously as much in the dark as everyone else. Mabel Beauford's husband neither knew nor cared what had happened to his wife, but he had given me the name of a friend of hers, Elizabeth Tagg. Unfortunately, every time I'd called her, I'd got no answer, and she didn't have voicemail.

It was such a strange way to die, and yet, there had now been three similar deaths in Candlefield recently. I'd spent the best part of two hours going through the archives of

The Candle to see if I could find any more cases, but with no success. Searching The Candle's archives was a laborious task. It made me even more determined to push the Combined Sup Council to reconsider their stance on the internet. It was absolutely ridiculous that there was no online access in Candlefield.

Next, I planned to see if I could find any similar cases in the human world. At least there, I had access to the internet. I searched on a variety of terms including: 'Die after laughing,' and 'Laughing death.' Eventually, I struck lucky when I searched for: 'Laughing causes heart failure.' I found a number of cases over the previous two years in various parts of the UK.

A man in Dover had laughed so much while at a football match, that he'd collapsed and died. An elderly woman in Pontypridd had been at her local knitting club when she'd started laughing for no apparent reason. Moments later, she was dead. The other cases all followed the same pattern. The person suddenly began laughing uncontrollably for no apparent reason. Moments later, they were dead.

I made a note of the various towns in which these incidents had taken place. One of them was in Tableford—twenty miles away. A few phone calls and a bit of expert P.I-ing later, and I'd found the name and address of the dead man's wife. The deceased was a Mr John Monroe; his widow was Carrie Monroe. I made a call, and she readily agreed to talk to me. She said I could go straight over there.

"Jules, I'm going out."

"Is it okay if I call Jethro while you're gone?"

"Yes, of course. Good luck."

Carrie Monroe was in her late forties. She was a pretty woman with bright blue eyes.

"I've been looking into deaths similar to that of your husband, and I wondered if perhaps I could talk to you about exactly what happened."

"Of course. Have a seat. Would you like a drink?"

"No, I'm fine, thanks. Perhaps you could start by telling me something about your husband?"

"John and I were very happy. He was a quiet man who kept himself to himself. He wasn't loud like some men. He was very hardworking. A postman, actually."

"Where was he when it happened?"

"We were together. We'd been out for the day to Lake Trinkle. Not actually on the lake. Just sitting by the side of it; watching the water. It was so peaceful—such a lovely day. Then, as we were about to come home, John started laughing. I couldn't understand why. John rarely laughed like that, even when he was watching something funny on TV. His laughter set me off. Laughing can be contagious, can't it? But he carried on and on, and I could see by his face that he was in some distress. Then, he collapsed. I called the ambulance, but he died before they arrived."

"What did they say was the cause of death?"

"They said his heart had given way. The strain of all the laughter had killed him."

"Had he been all right before that day?"

"Yes, he'd been fine. We'd been going about our daily life. In fact, only the night before, we'd been to see a band at the club down the road. The guitarist was an old friend of John's. We used to go and see his band whenever they played locally. We thoroughly enjoyed it. It was a lovely evening."

"He didn't complain of feeling ill then?"

"No, he was fine. There were no signs that anything was wrong at all."

***

I needed to find a snow globe that looked exactly the same as the one that Jack had bought for me. But how on earth was I going to do that? After I'd left Carrie Monroe's house, I checked online, and to my surprise and delight, I found there was a shop which specialised in snow globes just the other side of Washbridge. It was called Snow Limits, and they described themselves as the country's leading snow globe emporium. They apparently stocked thousands of snow globes. Maybe I'd be able to find something similar there.

The shop was on a small retail park, in between a furniture shop and a toy shop. The man behind the counter was wearing thick-rimmed glasses, which he took off when I approached him.

"Good afternoon. My name is Donny McDonald. How can I help you today?"

"You have an awful lot of snow globes."

"Yes, indeed. It's all we sell, hence the name: Snow Limits. Did you have a particular snow globe in mind? We have lots of different themes: romantic snow globes, scary snow globes, and even funny snow globes. This is one of the most popular at the moment." He lifted one up and showed it to me.

"Are those camels in there?"

"That's right." He shook the snow globe, so snow came

tumbling down onto the camels. "Hilarious, isn't it?"

Side-splitting. "I'm not really looking for a funny snow globe. Do you have any with houses in them?"

"Lots of them. You want aisle B."

There was shelf after shelf of snow globes with a variety of buildings inside them. Snow globes with churches, snow globes with town halls, snow globes with stadiums, and any number with houses of all shapes and sizes. But none of them looked anything like the one that Jack had bought me.

I went back to Donny McDonald.

"I haven't found anything suitable. Do you by any chance make custom snow globes? From a photograph, say?"

"We can, but I should warn you they're very expensive. They start at three hundred and fifty pounds."

"How much?" I surely hadn't heard him correctly.

"And that's the cheapest. I would have to see a photo before I could give you a firm price."

"I'll have to think about it."

I couldn't afford to pay that kind of money. I would just have to come clean, and tell Jack that I'd broken it. What else could I do? I couldn't tell him I'd sent it back to the supernatural world.

On the street outside my office, were seven young people—three women and four men—all dressed in shorts, and t-shirts with "I- Sweat" on the front. They were doing push ups and squats, and all manner of exercises. One of them offered me a leaflet.

"Can I interest you in this? It's for the new health club."

I took it from him. "Is it open?"

"Not yet, but they're accepting membership applications, so you can sign up today. It'll help you lose some of those excess pounds."

Excess pounds? Cheek.

Chapter 19

Jack had been up and out early doors. I'd slept in, and was running a little late. I hadn't had time for breakfast, so I called in at Coffee Triangle on my way to the office. As soon as I walked through the door, I knew something was amiss. There were lots of people crowded around the counter; they all seemed to be complaining. When I got closer, and could hear what was being said, it became apparent that the management had decided to introduce a woodwind day. And today was the first one.

Lots of customers had arrived expecting it to be gong day, and were very disappointed when they realised that they'd have to choose an instrument from the woodwind section.

"The only reason I came was because it was gong day," one man said.

"Me too. I like to get rid of all my tension by hitting a gong. I can hardly do that by playing a recorder, can I?"

"It's only a trial run." The young woman behind the counter was trying to placate them. "We're just trying it out for a couple of weeks to see what the reaction is."

"I can tell you my reaction." A young man wearing baggy jeans stepped forward. "I want a gong. I don't want a clarinet, thank you very much."

I eventually managed to order a flat white 'to go'.

Kathy was behind the counter in Ever, and already very busy. She had a queue of people waiting to pay. There was no point in my going inside because she wouldn't have had time to talk to me.

The shop across the road looked as though it was ready for opening, so I waited until the road was clear, and went to check it out. There was a display of seashells in the window. Inside the shop, I could see all manner of marine bric-a-brac. Suddenly, the name of the shop made perfect sense. 'She sells'—*She sells seashells.* There was only one person I could think of who would open a shop selling seashells, and that was none other than my old acquaintance, Betty Longbottom, the intrepid tax inspector.

The notice on the door read: *'Opening Tomorrow, 9:00.'*

***

Mrs V was hard at work knitting what was obviously a scarf. On the desk were two which she'd already finished. It was a long time since I'd seen her so absorbed in her knitting.

"Morning, Mrs V."

"Morning, Jill." She didn't even look up.

"You look very busy."

"I've got a deadline to meet. I have to knit twenty scarves by a week on Saturday. I'm not sure I'm going to make it."

"You could always get Jules to help you."

"Jules?" She stopped knitting for a second. "I assume that's a joke?"

"I thought you were teaching her."

"I am, but you saw the state of the scarf she's just knitted."

"It was a *little* uneven."

"That's the understatement of the year. She'll get there eventually, but I think it's going to take a year or two."

"Why the deadline for having the scarves finished?

What's the occasion?"

"They're for Armi. There's a fundraiser for the Cuckoo Clock Appreciation Society."

"I like the little cuckoo on each end of the scarves. That's clever."

"But very time-consuming. It's my own stupid fault. I should have given him some of those scarves out of the cupboard. But no, I had to suggest scarves with cuckoos on them. And not just that."

She held one up, and I could see the word 'cuckoo' had been knitted into the scarf.

"That's very nice."

"Thank you. I hope whoever buys these, appreciates the work that's gone into them."

Something about the cuckoo clock in my office didn't look right. I walked over to get a closer view, and then I realised what it was. There was parcel tape over the little door.

"Winky?"

"I'm busy!" The voice came from behind the screen.

"Come out here a minute."

"I've got to fit this accelerator."

"The accelerator will have to wait. Get your backside out here now!"

He appeared, holding a screwdriver and a spanner. "What is it? I'm very busy."

"What have you done to the clock?"

"I haven't done anything to it."

"What's this then?" I pulled off the parcel tape.

"Oh that? The stupid cuckoo kept waking me up every hour, so I had to do something to stop it. I didn't think you'd appreciate it if I smashed it again, so I put tape over the door to stop it popping out."

"And what exactly do you think Mrs V will say when she sees that?"

"The old bag lady hardly ever ventures in here. I don't think she likes me."

"I wonder why. Anyway, you can't leave the tape on the clock."

"How about I only put it on at night, so I can get some sleep? You don't want to see me sleep-deprived, do you?"

"Okay, but not until the office is closed, and Mrs V and I have gone home. And only on condition that you remove it before anyone arrives in the morning."

"Okay. Deal."

***

I was still very concerned about Jessica Lambeth. When she'd come to see me, she'd been worried about her boyfriend's behaviour. But other than that, she'd been bright enough. And yet, the other day when I'd gone to her flat, she'd seemed totally out of it—almost in a trance. She and her boyfriend were now *both* acting very strangely. I felt I owed it to her, as a client, to check that everything was okay, so I decided to pay her another visit.

When I got to her flat, I spotted Paul through the window, so I waited outside in the hope that he might leave, and allow me to speak to Jessica alone. I was out of luck because, three quarters of an hour later, they left together. They both still had the same trance-like look about them. I followed at a distance, even though they were so spaced-out that they probably wouldn't have noticed if I'd jumped out in front of them. It didn't take long to work out where they were headed. They were taking the same route to Bar Scarlet as Paul had taken when I'd followed him before.

I waited until they'd been in the bar for a few minutes, then followed them inside. Just as on my previous visit, the clientele was made up almost entirely of vampires. I made it inside just in time to see Paul and Jessica walk straight past the bar, and towards the back of the building where I'd lost Paul on the previous occasion. I was determined that wouldn't happen again, so I pushed my way through the crowd. I made it there just in time to see them go through a door, which I hadn't even noticed on my last visit. It was painted black, and set into a black wall. When the door was closed, you wouldn't have known it was there. Only when it opened, and light shone through from the room behind it, could you tell there was a door there at all.

As I got closer, two vampires blocked my way.

"Sorry, you can't go in there. It's private."

"But two friends of mine just went in."

"Sorry, no entry." They were both large men, and not exactly what you'd call friendly-looking. I could have used magic to get past them, but I wasn't sure it was appropriate. It could all have been quite innocent, and I didn't want to cause a scene unnecessarily.

I decided to leave the bar, and wait across the road until Paul and Jessica came out. A lot of people, mainly vampires, went in and out. The majority of the vampires stayed no more than a few minutes. The few humans who ventured inside seemed to stay much longer.

It was almost two hours later when Jessica and Paul re-emerged. If anything, they looked even worse than when they'd gone in. They seemed pale and tired, and were holding onto one another as though without each other's support, they would have collapsed. The two of them went straight back to Jessica's flat.

What was the attraction of Bar Scarlet? What was in the back room? And why did Jessica and Paul look so spaced-out? I would need to take a much closer look.

***

When I got back to the office, Mrs V was still hard at work on her scarves. Winky was also hard at work—on his *time machine*. Yeah, right!

I'd only been back for twenty minutes when I felt the familiar chill that told me a ghost was about to appear.

It was my father.

"Dad? I haven't seen you for a while."

"I know. I'm sorry. I've been rather busy. There was an unexpected turn of events."

"Nothing bad, I hope?"

"Quite the contrary. I've started seeing someone."

"That's great. Who is it?"

"Her name's Blodwyn."

"That's a very Welsh name, if ever there was one."

"Her mother is Welsh—hence the name. But her father is Italian. She was born and raised in Italy."

"I see. How did you and Blodwyn meet?"

"At my first NGS meeting."

"What's that?"

"The Novice Ghost Society. It's a support group for those struggling to adapt to being a ghost. I thought I might get a few tips there. It was Blodwyn's first visit too. In fact, she's the reason I've come to see you today."

"Oh?"

"I've told Blodwyn all about you, and she's keen to meet you. But I thought I should speak to you first, to see how you felt about it."

"I'd be delighted to meet her. Is she able to attach herself to the living yet?"

"She hasn't had the opportunity to try because her parents are both deceased, and she doesn't have any other family. Maybe the next time I come over, I could bring her to meet you."

"Sure. That would be great."

So, now I had a ghost mother who was married to a Welsh-Italian man named Alberto, and a ghost father who had recently started seeing an Italian-Welsh woman by the name of Blodwyn.

Nothing unusual there, then.

***

Jack wasn't home when I got back from work. There were no fresh molehills, and the existing ones were beginning to fade. It appeared my little chat with Mortimer had done the trick. I hadn't intended for him to go next door; I'd assumed he'd move into the fields behind. Poor Megan. Snigger.

I was still in the garden when Jack came home. When he spotted me through the window, he came out to join me.

"How was work today?" I asked.

"I have exciting news!" He had a big grin on his face.

"Did you get a promotion?"

"Much better. The guys at work have organised a bowling tournament."

"I thought you said it was exciting news?"

"It is. It's mixed doubles. So I thought that you and me—"

"Forget it!" I interrupted. "I'm not bowling."

"Why not?"

"Because it's boring. With a capital 'Y'."

"Huh?"

"'Y' for yawn."

"I seem to remember you enjoyed it when you beat me in the doubles."

"That was only because you'd set me up to lose. I was teaching you a lesson."

"Hello, you two."

"Hi, Megan." Jack beamed.

"Hi, Megan." I didn't beam.

"Did I hear you correctly, Jack?" she said. "Were you talking about a bowling tournament? Is that ten-pin bowling?"

"Is there any other kind?" Jack had a stupid grin on his face.

"I love ten-pin bowling," she gushed. "I used to play when I was younger, and I was pretty good, even if I do say so myself. I haven't played for a couple of years, but it's like riding a bike, isn't it? If Jill isn't interested, and you need a partner, I'd love to play."

"You're on," Jack said.

"Okay, I'd better get going." She started back to the house. "Let me know when you need me."

Chapter 20

When we got back in the house, Jack saw my expression. "What?"

"Don't give me 'what.' Why did you say she could partner you?"

"How could I say no? And besides, you weren't interested."

"You didn't try hard enough to persuade me."

"I shouldn't have to persuade you."

"You're impossible! I need custard creams."

To my horror, when I checked the cupboard, the Tupperware box was empty. Then I remembered; I'd eaten the last one the previous night. I'd intended to pick some up in Washbridge, but had forgotten all about it.

"I'm going to the corner shop," I said. "Do you want anything?"

"Will you get me some Marmite?"

"Yuk! How can you eat that horrible stuff?"

"It's lovely."

"Says you. I won't be long."

I was still fuming as I walked to the shop. I was mad at myself more than anything. Jack was right; it was my own stupid fault. I should have agreed to partner with him. I probably wouldn't have been so worried if Kathy hadn't put the idea into my head that I needed to watch Megan around Jack. Anyway, enough of that. The custard creams were calling.

There was no sign of Toby Jugg, the shop owner. A middle-aged woman was standing behind the counter. She had a face as long as a wet weekend.

I was amused to find that the shop was full of BOGOF signs. I'd been the one who had given Toby Jugg the idea of using them.

"Hello there," I said.

She grunted something unintelligible.

"Isn't Toby in today?"

"I'm Judy—his wife. Toby's gone fishing, and left me in charge of the shop. Again!"

"I see you have a lot of BOGOF deals."

"Don't mention those to me. I'm sick of all the offers. He's had me making signs every hour of the day. BOGOF this and BOGOF that. Some stupid woman came in here, and gave him the idea."

Whoops!

"Aren't the promotions working?"

"Oh yes, they've been a great success, but I've got better things to do than make stupid signs. I had to cancel my Zumba class this week."

I went straight to the aisle where Toby kept the custard creams, but to my dismay, there were none on the shelf.

"I'm after some custard creams, Judy, but there aren't any on the shelf."

"There's a box full on the top there—above the shelving, but I can't reach them."

"Don't you have a ladder?"

"It broke."

"Right, okay." I wasn't sure I believed her—it was much more likely to be a case of chronic laziness.

There was no way I was going back empty-handed—I had to have custard creams. I waited until I was sure Judy wasn't watching, and then levitated until I was high enough to reach the box. It was rather heavy, but I managed to lower myself and the box back to the ground.

"There you go." I put it on the counter. "I managed to reach them."

She gave me a puzzled look which was hardly surprising as the shelving was at least seven feet high.

"I suppose I'd better put some out then. How many packets did you want?"

"Two, no make that three. And a pot of your finest Marmite, please."

***

Jack had gone to work before I woke up the next morning. It was just as well because I'd been dreaming about him and Megan. If he'd still been home, I would have given him a real tongue-lashing for flirting, even if it was only in my dreams.

I called Jules and told her that I probably wouldn't be in, and asked her to let me know if there were any important calls. As I was speaking to her, I could hear the sound of knitting needles. She was getting as bad as Mrs V.

I planned to stake out Bar Scarlet. Something weird was going on in there, and whatever it was, it seemed to have affected both Paul and Jessica. I felt sure the answer was to be found in the room behind the black door.

I got there just before ten o'clock, but nothing much happened until midday. From then, there was a steady stream of people in and out of the bar. As before, the majority of them were vampires. The few humans who entered the bar had one thing in common; they all had the same spaced-out look as Paul and Jessica. And they all seemed even more disoriented when they came out.

By mid-afternoon, I'd seen enough. It was time to take a closer look. I waited until the next human arrived. It turned out to be a man in his thirties; he too had the same spaced-out look as all the others. I made myself invisible, then hurried across the road, and followed him into the bar.

It was much quieter than on my last two visits. The man made his way towards the back of the bar. I followed. The vampires, who had blocked my way on the previous occasion, stepped aside to let him pass, and I slipped in with him.

On the other side of the black door was what appeared to be some kind of laboratory. The walls, the floor and the ceiling were all white. I followed the man down a short corridor, at the end of which, he took the door on the right.

We were now in a large room with beds all around the walls. Lying on the beds were humans—some male, some female. Protruding from their arms were tubes, and flowing through those tubes was a red liquid. Someone was taking their blood.

Two vampires, dressed in white smocks, were going from bed to bed, checking each of the humans in turn. Another vampire greeted the young man who I'd just followed. The vampire led him to one of the vacant beds, and proceeded to insert a tube into his arm. All of the tubes fed into a single large tank at the far end of the room.

This was a feeding house for vampires!

I had to wait a further fifteen minutes until one of the humans was allowed to leave. A woman, in her late twenties, was unhooked from the tube, and helped off the bed. She looked completely out of it, and was a little unsteady on her feet. I followed her to the door, and slipped out behind her.

Still invisible, I made my way over to the bar. Just as I'd suspected, the majority of the vampires were drinking blood on tap. Once sated, they simply left the bar.

I had to let Daze know, so as soon as I outside, and a safe distance from the bar, I made myself visible again and called her.

"Daze, it's Jill."

"Jill, I'm sorry. I can't talk at the moment. We're on the tracks of a rogue werewolf."

"Okay. Call me as soon as you can, will you?"

***

On my way back to the office, I noticed that 'She Sells' was now open, so I crossed the road to get a closer look. There, behind the counter, was a familiar face—one I hadn't seen for almost six months.

Betty Longbottom looked very different from the last time I'd seen her. She'd shed the dowdy tax inspector look, and was now every inch the hippy. Her assistants were attending to the customers, so I managed to catch Betty's eye.

"Jill! Long time, no see."

"Hi, Betty. This is something of a departure for you, isn't it?"

"It was time for a change. No one loves a tax inspector, as I'm sure you're aware, so I decided to follow my dreams. When I saw this shop was free, it was like a sign."

"You must be very excited."

"I am. It's a new beginning."

"I was sorry to hear that you and Luther have gone your separate ways."

What? Who are you calling a hypocrite?

"Don't talk to me about that man. He had the audacity to accuse me of stealing one of his seashells. As if I would stoop so low."

As if? This was the woman who had been shoplifting for years.

The queue of customers now stretched back to the door.

"I'd better let you go, Betty. I can see you're busy. Good luck with your new venture."

"Thanks, Jill. Do pop in again."

I was almost back at the office when I got a call. It was Daze.

"Jill, I'm sorry I couldn't speak earlier, but I didn't want to spook the werewolf."

"Did you get him?"

"Yes, he's banged up in Candlefield. What was it you wanted to talk to me about?"

"Can we meet somewhere?"

"How about Cuppy C in ten minutes?"

"Okay, I'll see you there."

When I arrived at Cuppy C, Laura and Flora were working behind the counter in the cake shop. The twins were in the tea room.

"Hi, Jill," Amber said. "Guess what. We're going to get a new sign for Cuppy C."

"Why? There's nothing wrong with the one you've got."

"We need a change."

"Signs can be very expensive, you know."

"Ah, but that's where you're wrong. We're going to pick one up for a song."

"How are you going to manage that?"

"Voila!" Amber dropped a small catalogue on the table.

"Signs by phone?" I picked it up. "How's that work, exactly."

"They have tons of different styles. You pick one, measure how big you want it, and then phone your order through. That's why they can do them so cheap."

"I'm not sure about this." I flicked through the brochure—there was no denying they had a comprehensive range of styles.

"Why not?" Amber said.

"What happens if you get the measurements wrong?"

"We're not stupid, Jill!" Pearl sounded affronted.

"I know that, but it's easy to make a mistake."

"We'll check and double-check before we phone the order through."

"Don't you think it might be better to get the professionals in?"

"These are professionals. Just look at the signs they make."

"Okay. Just don't come crying to me if it all goes wrong."

"Nothing will go wrong. You're just a pessimist." Amber huffed. "Did you want something to drink, or are you just here to pour cold water on our plans?"

Sting!

"I'm meeting Daze in a few minutes. I'll have one of your small blueberry muffins, please."

"You know we only have the one size. Large."

"Oh well. That will have to do, I suppose. I see you've got Laura and Flora working in the cake shop."

"They're doing a great job."

"Hmm?"

"Why are you so down on those two?" Pearl asked.

"You've really got it in for them." Amber passed me a muffin.

"I don't trust them. Not since that day when they were smoking and drinking upstairs. And I've seen them talking to Miles and Mindy. Just keep an eye on them—that's all I'm saying."

I'd no sooner sat down than Daze arrived. She came straight over to join me.

"What is it, Jill? It sounded urgent."

"I was recently hired by a woman to follow her boyfriend. She was worried because he'd been acting strange. Anyway, to cut a long story short, I've discovered some kind of vampire feeding den."

"What do you mean?"

"They're taking human blood, and selling it in a bar called Bar Scarlet."

"You've actually seen this?"

"Yes. There's some kind of lab in the back where they take the blood. It's then sold on tap in the bar."

"This is really serious. What about the humans? Are they being killed?"

"No. Once the blood has been taken, they're allowed back onto the streets. But they look completely out of it."

"They must be drugging them."

"That's what I thought. Why else would they keep going back there?"

"Are you sure about all of this?"

"I'm positive. I've seen it with my own eyes."

"This is terrible. It happened once before about ten years ago, but we thought we'd put a stop to it. I can't understand how this has happened without us knowing. We usually have good intel on this sort of thing."

"What are you going to do?"

"Shut them down, and quickly. I need to get moving on this right away."

Chapter 21

"Do you think Mrs Mopp would iron my shirts?" Jack said, the next morning over breakfast.

"Why can't you iron your own shirts?"

"I can. But I thought if we're paying her anyway, and she has a bit of time left, maybe she could iron my shirts as well."

"If you want Mrs Mopp to iron your shirts, you can ask her. I'm not doing it."

"You sound like you're scared of her."

"You haven't met her yet, have you? I tell you what, the next time she comes in, why don't you have a word with her? Ask her if she'd like to iron your shirts."

"I will. I'm not scared of a cleaning lady."

"Good for you. Good luck, buddy."

He put a large spoonful of mushy corn flakes into his mouth, and then mumbled something unintelligible.

"I'm sorry? Was that English?"

He eventually managed to swallow the corn flake mush. "I said, Kathy's taking a long time making her mind up about the snow globe, isn't she?'"

"She said she wanted to show it to Peter and the kids before making a decision."

"It's a wonder Kathy ever gets anything done. If it takes her this long to make her mind up whether she wants a snow globe, how on earth did she and Peter ever decide to get married and have kids?"

"Kathy can be a bit scatter-brained. Don't worry about it. I'll give her a call to remind her."

What was I going to do about the stupid snow globe? If Snow Limit didn't have it, I was never going to find one, and it was way too expensive to have one custom made. The only other option was to shrink one of the houses in Candlefield, and put it in a globe.

What? I was only joking. Of course I wouldn't do anything like that. Sheesh! What do you take me for?

When I glanced out of the front window, I spotted Mr Hosey coming down the road on his silly little train. He pulled up outside our house, walked to the back carriage, took out one of the train-stops, and plonked it smack bang in the centre of our driveway, just as he'd done before. Right! I'd show him! When he started towards the cab, I cast the 'move' spell, and the train-stop gradually slid down the road until it was clear of our driveway.

He was about to climb into the cab when he glanced back, and did a double-take. I ducked down so he wouldn't see me. When I looked up again, he was moving the train-stop back in front of our driveway. As soon as he started back to the cab, I did the same again. This time, when he saw the sign had moved, he looked up and down the road, trying to figure out who had done it. Once again, I ducked out of sight. When I looked up this time, he'd climbed into the cab. He'd obviously admitted defeat. Moments later he set off down the street.

As I drove into Washbridge, I noticed a bus coming in the opposite direction. By now, I was used to seeing Grandma's advertisements everywhere, but there was something different about this one. Where it should have said, 'Ever A Wool Moment,' it now said, 'Never A Wool Moment.' And below the name, it read, 'Too expensive. Poor quality. We hate our customers.'

What was that all about?

As I continued my journey, I kept my eyes peeled for more buses or taxis. Every one I saw carried the same advert. Could it be some kind of perverse marketing campaign by Grandma? Was it reverse psychology? No, this looked more like sabotage to me. Someone had changed the adverts. Grandma would go crazy when she found out.

As I stepped into my office building, I bumped into Brent and George from I-Sweat.

"Hi, guys."

"Hello there," Brent said.

"Hi, Jill." George flashed me a smile.

"How's it going, you two? When do you open?"

"It won't be long now," George said. "We'd still like to take over your office. I don't suppose there's anything we can do to change your mind, is there?"

"No. I've already given you my reasons."

"Fair enough." George shrugged. "Is there any chance we could get you to take your name off the door?"

"Why would I do that?"

"We thought you could put *'Private – Staff only'* on it instead. That way our customers would think it was part of the health club."

"And how would new clients find me?"

"Hmm? I hadn't thought about that."

It was supposed to be Mrs V's day in, but both she and Jules were sitting at her desk—both knitting as if their lives depended on it.

"Morning, you two. I wasn't expecting to see you today, Jules."

"I decided to come in to help Mrs V. She has to get these scarves ready for Armi's fundraiser."

"That's very kind of you, isn't it, Mrs V?"

"Very." Mrs V rolled her eyes, and then followed me through to my office.

"You have to send her home, Jill."

"But, I thought she was helping you?"

"Helping? She keeps asking *me* to help *her* because she drops a stitch every five minutes. I'm never going to get anything done at this rate."

"You can't throw kindness back in her face."

"I know, but she's driving me insane. It's not just the dropped stitches. She's been talking nonstop about her new young man. Jed or Jeff or something like that."

"Do you mean Jethro?"

"That's him. From what I can gather, he's asked her out on a first date. Don't you just hate young love?"

After she'd got everything off her chest, Mrs V went back to the outer office. All the time I'd been talking to her I could hear noises coming from behind the screen. Winky was obviously still hard at work on his time machine.

"How's it going, Winky?" I popped my head around the screen.

"I'm just putting the final touches to it. Anytime now, it'll be finished."

"I hope you've got your money ready for when it proves to be another of your disasters."

"We'll see. You'll be laughing on the other side of your face soon."

At least Winky had remembered to remove the parcel tape from the door of the cuckoo clock. It was just as well because if Mrs V had seen it, I would have got it in the neck.

***

The next name on my list of people, living in the human world, who had died from laughing was a Chrissy Knowles. She'd lived in Lansdale which was over a hundred miles from Washbridge. It wasn't worth my while to drive over there, but I'd managed to get her phone number, so I called her widower.

"Is that Dominic Knowles?"

"Speaking."

"I'm sorry to bother you. My name is Jill Gooder. I'm a private investigator. One of the cases I've been working on has led me to look at the recent spate of deaths from laughing. I understand your wife, Chrissy, died that way."

"That's right, she did."

"Would you mind if I asked you a few questions?"

"Of course not. I'll help if I can."

"Was she normally the sort of person who laughed out loud?"

"Chrissy? No, not at all. She was a very quiet woman. Very shy. She had a lovely smile, but rarely laughed."

"What about in the days prior to her death? Had anything out of the ordinary happened? Had she shown any sign of illness?"

"No, nothing like that. In fact, only the night before she died, we went to the local club. Chrissy wasn't keen. She wasn't a big fan of comedians."

"A comedian? You don't happen to remember his name, do you?"

"Yes, it was a man called Lenny Hope. I thought he was hilarious. So did everyone in the place except Chrissy. She didn't laugh, and said afterwards that she hadn't found him funny. The next day, I got a phone call at work. Chrissy had been at the hairdresser when she suddenly started laughing for no reason at all—laughing hysterically. The next thing, she collapsed and died."

"I'm very sorry to have brought back such bad memories, Mr Knowles."

"That's all right. Is there a reason you're asking these questions? Is there something suspicious about these deaths?"

"It's too early to say, but I promise I'll keep you posted."

Chrissy Knowles had been to see a comedian the day before she died, and so had Gloria Cloverleaf. That warranted further investigation, so I searched online for Lenny Hope, and found his website. He was a strange-looking man with long, curly hair. He was wearing sunglasses in the photograph. Also on the website were details of all the cities and towns where he'd played over the last two years. They included Dover and Pontypridd—two of the towns where people had died from laughing. Normally, that would have pointed to some kind of connection, but when I'd spoken to Carrie Monroe about her husband, John, she'd told me that they'd been to see a band, not a comedian.

I gave her a call.

"Carrie, it's Jill Gooder. I came to see you the other day."

"Oh yes. Hi, Jill."

"Look, can I double-check something you told me? You said the night before your husband died, you'd been to see a band. Did I get that right?"

"Yeah. Why?"

"I'm just following a few leads. I thought I might be onto something, but maybe not."

"Yeah, we got there earlier than planned, and caught a bit of the opening act. A comedian."

"You don't remember his name, do you?"

"Not offhand. I thought he was really funny. John didn't."

"It wasn't Lenny Hope, was it?"

"That's him."

"Thanks, Carrie. Thanks very much."

I took a closer look at the photo of Lenny Hope. The pieces were now starting to slot into place, but to be absolutely sure, I would need to speak to Elizabeth Tagg, Mabel Beauford's friend. I gave her another call with little or no expectation of her answering.

"Hello?"

"Is that Elizabeth Tagg?"

"Yes, speaking."

"Hi. My name is Jill Gooder. I'm—"

"You're the level seven witch, aren't you?"

"Sort of. Look, I'm sorry to bother you, but I understand you were a friend of Mabel Beauford?"

"That's right. Mabel and I had been friends since we were teenagers. Such a tragedy."

"Her husband gave me your number."

"That waste of space? I don't know why Mabel didn't leave him. I'd told her she could move in with me, but she was too proud to accept my help. Anyway, what did you want to speak to me about?"

"I understand you and Mabel went out the night before she died."

"That's right, we did. That's what I don't understand. She seemed fine that night."

"Could I ask where you went?"

"We went to see a comedian at Candlefield Social. I thought it might cheer Mabel up, but she barely cracked a smile all night."

Eureka!

***

When I arrived at Cuppy C there was a long queue outside the door. It took me a few seconds to work out that the doors were locked. That's when I spotted the sign:

Sups Eat Free

I burst out laughing, but then spotted Amber and Pearl staring at me, stony-faced, from inside the shop. Amber gestured for me to go around to the back entrance.

"It's not funny, Jill." Amber snapped after she'd let me in.

"I know. I'm sorry. No one knows better than me how problematic signage can be."

"I can't believe they did it." Amber shook her head in disbelief. "Why would we call the shop 'Sups Eat Free'?"

"How on earth did it happen?"

"The man on the phone was as deaf as a post. He must have taken down the name wrong."

"Didn't he read it back to you?"

"Actually, I didn't speak to him."

I looked at Pearl.

"I didn't speak to him either."

"So who did order the sign?"

"We had to go out," Pearl said. "We needed new shoes for our housewarming parties. We left the order with Flora and Laura to phone through."

"Where are they, anyway?"

"We sent them home when we closed the shop."

"Why did you close the shop?"

"Because everyone who came in expected to eat for free."

"What did Laura and Flora say about the cock-up?"

"They were the ones who told us that the man on the order line had been hard of hearing."

Alarm bells were starting to ring.

"Why didn't you stop them putting the sign up when you saw their mistake?"

"We weren't in when they came to install it. We were shopping for handbags."

"For the housewarming parties?"

"Precisely."

"Surely, Flora and Laura were in?"

"They were, but they were busy serving customers. They didn't see the sign until it was up, and by then the men had left."

"Presumably, you've told the signage people to come and take it down?"

"Of course we have," Pearl said. "But they can't come until tomorrow, so we have to keep the shop closed all day. It's going to cost us a fortune."

I decided against having a drink.

On my way out of Cuppy C, I bumped into three familiar characters, who I'd hoped never to see again: Ma Chivers, Alicia and Cyril.

"Hello, Jill," Ma said.

"I haven't seen the three of you for a while. Where have you been?"

"Wouldn't you like to know?" She sneered.

"No, not really."

"We didn't feel the need to *advertise* the fact that we're back." The three of them laughed, and then carried on down the street. What was that all about? *'We didn't feel the need to advertise?'* – Grandma's advertising! It must have been Ma Chivers who'd sabotaged it.

Chapter 22

Mid-morning the next day, Jessica Lambeth turned up at my office unannounced.

"I hope you don't mind me popping in like this, Jill."

"Not at all, come in."

She looked much better than on the last two occasions I'd seen her. Her eyes were bright again, and she no longer looked spaced-out.

"Are you okay now, Jessica?"

"Yeah, I feel so much better. I don't know what came over me these last few days. I've been really out of it. And it isn't just me. Paul's back to his old self too. We're getting on so much better now. I don't know what happened. Maybe we've had some sort of virus?"

"Could be. Whatever it was, it seemed to knock you both for six. I'm glad you're feeling better."

"Me too. You must let me have your bill for the work you did. I know it turned out to be a waste of time in the end, but I don't care. All that matters is I've got the old Paul back. Thanks again, Jill."

She turned to leave.

"One last thing, Jessica."

"Yeah?"

"Have you ever heard of a bar called Bar Scarlet?"

"No, I can't say I have. Why?"

"No reason. Thanks again for coming in. I'll post my bill out to you."

Winky came out from behind the screen.

"Ta-dah!" he said.

"Ta-dah what?"

"I've finished. The time machine is complete."

This should be interesting.

He pulled back the screen to reveal the finished product. It was much bigger than I'd expected—almost as tall as I was.

"It's rather big isn't it? It will never get off the ground."

"You really don't know anything about time travel, do you?"

"Go on then. Enlighten me."

"The machine doesn't move. It projects whoever's inside it through time."

"That's not how it should work."

"Says who?"

"I've seen the movies and TV programmes."

"You do realise they aren't real?" Winky sighed.

"And *this* is?"

"Absolutely."

"Okay. Whatever you say. I don't know why I'm wasting my breath arguing with you when you're obviously a spanner short of a toolbox. I just hope you've got your money ready to pay out on the bet."

"Don't count your hens."

"Chickens."

"What?"

"It's don't count your chickens."

"Hens? Chickens? Same difference. Would you like to accompany me on the maiden voyage?"

"Me? Get in that thing? No chance!"

"Are you scared?"

"Yeah, petrified." There were all sorts of lights and dials on the side of the metal cabinet. Inside it was a single large lever. "You're not getting me in there!"

"Wouldn't you like to travel through time?"

"That would be great, but until somebody invents a time machine, I guess I'm stuck here."

"The machine you're waiting for is right here in front of you."

"That remains to be seen. So where in time will you be travelling to, exactly?"

"I have absolutely no idea. The machine doesn't work like that. I can't dial in a date; it's just pot-luck. It may be sometime in the future, or back in the past. That's part of the excitement. Surely, you want to be involved?"

"No. I'm good, thanks."

"Your loss." He stepped into the cabinet. "Are you sure? This is your last chance."

"I'm positive. Just make sure you've got your money ready to pay me."

He pushed the lever, and the cabinet began to vibrate. Lights flashed on and off, and steam rose slowly from the outlets on the side, obscuring the cabinet.

"Winky, are you all right?"

The cabinet carried on vibrating for a couple of minutes, and then suddenly, it stopped. The lights stopped flashing, and slowly, the steam cleared. There was no sign of Winky. The cabinet was empty.

"Winky, where are you? Winky?"

He was nowhere to be seen. I didn't see how he could have got out of the cabinet without me seeing him. I checked under my desk and under the sofa, but there was no sign of him.

"Winky, where are you?"

Suddenly, the door to the outer office opened, and I almost jumped out of my skin.

"Jill, are you okay?" Jules was looking at me as though I'd gone crazy.

"Yes, I'm fine. I've just lost the cat."

"Where's he gone?"

"I don't know, Jules. That's why he's lost."

"Sorry. Maybe he got out of the window?"

It was slightly ajar.

"Yeah, I suppose he must have."

"What's that thing?" Jules was looking at the time machine.

"That—err—that's a sort of experimental—err—lie detector."

"It's very big for a lie detector, isn't it?"

"It's a new kind. Instead of having wires attached to your arm, you simply step inside it. When you answer questions, the lights flash if you're not telling the truth."

"How very clever. But why do you need one?"

"I'm testing it for a friend."

"Can I give it a try?"

"No, sorry. It isn't ready yet. There's a lot more testing to be done on it."

I spent the next ten minutes looking for Winky, but he was nowhere to be found. This had to be some kind of elaborate trick. He'd probably sneaked out the window when I wasn't looking.

I couldn't hang around there all day waiting for him to turn up, so I magicked myself over to Aunt Lucy's house. It was like deja-vu. She and Lester were arguing again.

"Hi, Aunt Lucy. Is it okay for me to come in?"

"Of course. Take no notice of us."

"I was just on my way out, anyway." Lester started for

the door. "It's no good me trying to talk to Lucy while she's in this mood."

"I take it he still wants to go ahead with the Grim Reaper application?" I said, after he'd left.

"It's far worse than that." Aunt Lucy took a seat at the kitchen table. "He's actually been offered the job."

"As a Grim Reaper?"

"Yes."

"Is he going to take it?"

"He says so. I've told him it's a ridiculous idea, but what do I know? He won't listen to me. Anyway, never mind that. Have you any news on Gloria Cloverleaf?"

"Nothing concrete yet, but I do have a hunch which I need to follow up on. I may know more later today."

Aunt Lucy and I had tea and cupcakes. By the time I was ready to leave, she was much brighter.

"Hopefully, when Lester comes back, he will have seen sense," she said.

I didn't say so, but I was pretty sure that Lester would take the job. He didn't want to be out of work, and unable to bring any money in. Hopefully, the job would work out for him, and Aunt Lucy would come around in time.

The twins were behind the tea-room counter in Cuppy C.

"I see you've got your old sign back up."

"Thank goodness." Pearl looked mightily relieved.

"Yes, but we're still getting complaints," Amber said. "You wouldn't believe how many people have asked if everything is still free. They're such children."

"Have the signage people agreed to make a replacement?"

"No, because they still insist that they provided exactly what we ordered."

I glanced over at the cake counter. Flora and Laura were there, and they seemed to be giggling about something.

Hmm?

Daze had arranged to meet me for a coffee. She arrived five minutes later.

"Thanks for the tip-off about Bar Scarlet, Jill. I don't know how that one slipped under our radar. It was one of the biggest operations of its kind."

"Have you closed it down?"

"Yes. All those involved have been arrested, and are behind bars in Candlefield. They won't see the light of day for a long time. It's one of the worst crimes imaginable—providing human blood for vampires in the human world."

"What will happen to Bar Scarlet?"

"It's been boarded up, and we've removed all the blood transfusion equipment so no one else can get hold of it. But of course, there's going to be a knock-on effect."

"How do you mean?"

"They'd been operating out of there for quite some time, and had a large clientele, as you probably noticed."

"Yeah, I saw a lot of vampires going in and out."

"Exactly. Those vampires have been getting a regular supply of fresh human blood for goodness knows how long. Now we've turned off the tap, do you think they'll all simply shrug their shoulders, and go back to synthetic blood?"

"I hadn't thought of that."

"Hopefully, most of them will. But there are bound to be some who can't shake the craving for human blood. If they can't get it on tap—it doesn't bear thinking about."

"That could be bad news for the people of Washbridge, couldn't it?"

"Very. I've sent extra Rogue Retrievers over there to keep an eye on events. If you see anything, let us know. It could be very dangerous for humans in Washbridge just now."

***

After Daze had left, I spent some time in my room above Cuppy C. Then, in the evening, I made my way to Candlefield Social. I was one of the first to arrive. It was the last night of Kenny Pope's run. I managed to nab a good seat right at the front, and ordered myself a ginger beer. I'd been tempted to order something stronger, but I wanted to keep my wits about me.

Slowly but surely, the club filled up. The punters were obviously looking forward to the night's entertainment. I could hear a lot of them saying that they'd heard very good reports about Kenny Pope.

Ten minutes before the show was due to start, I spotted the comedian in the wings. Just as I'd suspected, he was casting a spell on the audience. But I was ready for him.

A few minutes later, Kenny Pope walked onto the stage. He went straight into his routine. It was the same one I'd heard him practising the other day. The jokes were terrible, but this time I wasn't the only one who thought so. The audience sat, stony-faced. You could have heard a pin drop. After the punchline of the first gag, only a couple of people laughed. There was a look of concern on Pope's face. He carried on. His next joke was met with stony silence. After the third joke, people were getting restless.

"Rubbish!" someone at the back shouted.

"You're not funny!" a man on the front row yelled.

"Get off!"

After each joke, more and more people began to heckle him. Someone threw something on stage. It looked like a half-eaten apple. The shouts of, *'Get off!'* were getting louder. In the end, he had no option but to leave the stage. I almost felt sorry for the man.

I made my way backstage, and found him in his dressing room, which was no more than a glorified cupboard. He was in a chair, with his head in his hands.

"What do you want?" He looked up.

"I'd like a quick chat about your performance tonight."

"Come to gloat? Well you can get out! Leave me alone."

"Wouldn't you like to know why your act went down like a lead balloon tonight, Kenny?"

"Who are you? What do you mean?"

"It was because I blocked your spell."

He looked at me more intently. "What are you talking about?"

"Just what I said. I blocked the spell that you've been using to make people laugh at your jokes—to make people think you're funny. Tonight, the audience saw and heard you for what you really are. You're not funny, Kenny. You're not a comedian."

"Why would you do that?"

"Because the spell you've been using is dangerous. It's killing people. But you already know that. It happened in the human world, and now it's happening here."

"That's just a coincidence. It has nothing to do with

me."

"It has everything to do with you! The spell works just fine on most people; it makes them laugh at your jokes. But for those people who rarely laugh out loud, the effect of the spell can be delayed by up to a day. And then, when it finally kicks in, it does so with devastating effect. You must have realised that, so why didn't you stop?"

"You have no proof of any of this."

"There's plenty of proof. For a start, there's all the people in the human world who died laughing after they'd been to your gig."

"I don't know what you mean. I've never worked in the human world."

"Not under your real name, perhaps."

"Not under any name."

"Come on, Kenny. Or should I call you Lenny? The curly hair and sunglasses isn't fooling anyone."

I could see in his eyes that he knew the game was up.

"Is that why you came back to the sup world? Were you hoping the spell wouldn't have such a devastating effect on sups? If so, you were wrong. Three people have died so far, and all because you wanted to make the audience laugh."

"Who are you anyway? What's it got to do with you?"

"I'm Jill Gooder, and I'll tell you what it's got to do with me. I won't stand by and see people die just because you want them to think you're funny."

Just then, the door behind me opened, and in walked Maxine Jewell with two uniformed officers.

"Is this him?" She looked at me for confirmation.

"Yes, this is your man."

"Kenny Pope, I'm arresting you."

"What for?"

"You're charged with causing death by the reckless use of magic." She handcuffed him, and led him away.

"It's okay, Maxine," I shouted after her. "There's no need for a thank you."

Chapter 23

I recognised that cough. It was a Winky cough. When I looked up from my desk, there he was, standing in front of the so-called time machine.

"Where have you been?"

"Time travelling, of course."

"Don't be ridiculous. Where were you hiding?"

"I wasn't hiding anywhere. I've travelled in time, and now I'm back."

"And you really expect me to believe that?"

"I knew you wouldn't, that's why I've brought something back with me which will prove I'm telling the truth."

"Oh yeah? And what's that?"

"Something you may recognise." He put a book on my desk—a children's book.

"What's this?"

"Take a closer look."

I did as he asked, and it did indeed look familiar. My adoptive father had given me an identical book when I was a young child. I'd loved that book. And I mean *'really'* loved it. It was a picture story book about animals. When you pressed the buttons on the pages, it was supposed to make a noise like an animal, but in reality it just made squeaking noises, which is why I used to call it 'squeaky book.'

I would often go to work with Dad during the school holidays. He always asked Kathy if she wanted to come too, but she never did. She and her friends were too busy playing with their Barbies. While he was working, I'd play with my toys in the office. I often brought squeaky book with me, even though I knew Dad didn't like it. He used to say the noise got on his nerves, and stopped him concentrating.

"Tell me what really happened, Winky. Where did you get this?"

"I've already told you. I have no control over where the time machine sends me. This time it sent me back just a few years to this very office. You were playing just over there." He pointed to the corner of the room, which is where I used to play—near the sofa.

"So you're saying you actually saw me?"

"Yes. Well, a mini-you. You were quite pretty as a young child. What went wrong?"

"Cut the cheek. What happened exactly?"

"Mini-you really liked me. So much so, you insisted on giving me your book."

"This is total nonsense."

"Is that your book or not?"

I flipped through the pages. Every one of them was familiar; I could remember them all. I pressed the buttons, and the book squeaked. But that still didn't mean it was my book. Winky must have somehow found out about squeaky book, and got hold of a copy.

But then, I turned the final page, and there was my name, written in a young child's handwriting. I could remember writing it. This *was* my book. It was 'squeaky book.'

"Do you believe me now?" Winky jumped onto my desk.

"Yes—err—no—err. I don't know what to believe."

"You saw your name, right? You know it's the genuine article."

"Did you see my dad while you were there?"

"He'd just stepped out. I think he was in the outer office with someone. I could hear voices out there."

"Why didn't you wait for him to come back into the office?"

"And how do you think that would have played out? I'm a time-travelling cat. How was I supposed to explain that to him? It's not like he could have understood me anyway. He wasn't a sup, remember?"

"So you just talked to mini-me?"

"That's right. We chatted while you were playing in the corner, and then you gave me squeaky book. Anyway, on to more important issues. I think you'll agree that I've proved beyond a shadow of a doubt that this is indeed a time machine."

What could I say? He'd brought back squeaky book. How else could he have done it other than by travelling back in time?

"I suppose so."

"Good. Well, in that case, there's just the small matter of making good on the bet. We said two hundred pounds, I believe?"

"I'll have to write you a cheque."

"No cheques." He passed me a slip of paper.

"What's this?"

"It's my account number and sort code. You can make a bank transfer."

"Okay." I brought up my online banking, and authorised the transfer of two hundred pounds to Winky's account. I was so stunned it didn't even occur to me to ask how a cat had managed to open a bank account.

"Winky, if this machine of yours really does work—"

"What do you mean, *'If it works'*? I've proven it does."

"Okay. In that case, maybe I could try it too?"

"There's a slight problem there. The machine can't be operated too often. We'll need to wait awhile before we can use it again."

"How long?"

"At least a week."

"That long?"

"That's just the way it is. A time machine is a very complex piece of kit. These things can't be rushed."

"Okay, but then I want to go back in time with you. I'd love to see my dad again."

"We can try, but like I said before, I can't guarantee where or when we'll end up."

***

My mind was still spinning with thoughts of time travel as I made my way to Ever A Wool Moment. I wanted to let Grandma know about her advertising.

"Are you all right?" Grandma said when I walked into the back office.

"Yeah. I'm fine."

"Are you sure? You look a bit—I don't know—not quite with it."

"I'm okay. Do you believe in time travel, Grandma?"

"Of course I don't. Why?"

"No reason. Look, I wanted to see you because I bumped into Ma Chivers, Alicia, and Cyril near Cuppy C."

"I was beginning to hope those three had disappeared for good, along with all the other wicked witches."

"No such luck. It seems they're back."

"Okay, but you didn't need to make a special journey to tell me that."

"There's something else. Someone is sabotaging your advertising."

"What do you mean sabotaging it?"

"Someone has changed the ads to read 'Never A Wool Moment,' and added lots of derogatory comments."

Her face turned red with rage, and her wart looked as though it might explode at any moment.

"Who did it? Do you know?"

"I don't have any proof, but when I bumped into Ma Chivers, she said something weird. She said, she didn't feel the need to 'advertise' the fact that they were back in Candlefield, and she emphasised the word *'advertise.'* Then all three of them laughed. I didn't clock it at the time, but as soon as they'd gone, I realised she might have been dropping a not too subtle hint about what she'd done."

"Thanks for telling me, Jill. I'll sort this out. Ma Chivers will be laughing on the other side of her face when I've finished with her."

"Don't do anything rash."

"Rash? That's a good idea. I'll give them a rash—all three of them. A very itchy rash."

"Okay, well I'd better get back to the office."

"Before you go, is it true what I've heard about Fester?"

"It's Lester."

"Whatever. A little bird told me he's going to be working as a Grim Reaper."

"That's right, but Aunt Lucy isn't very happy about it."

"Whyever not? If ever a man was cut out to be a Grim

Reaper, then Fester is that man."

***

As soon as I got back to the office, Mrs V collared me.

"There was a man here to see you. You've only just missed him."

"Why didn't you ask him to wait?"

"I did. I told him you wouldn't be long, but he said he couldn't hang around. He seemed rather nervous. He said his name was Damon, and that you knew him."

"What did he look like?"

"He was tall, with red hair and a red beard."

Back at my desk, I racked my brain for anyone called Damon, but drew a blank. The description Mrs V had given me, matched that of the man who had called at my house. That man had talked to me as though I was a long-lost friend, but as far as I could remember, I'd never seen him before in my life.

Just then, a chill fell over the office. I was in contact with so many ghosts now, I wasn't sure which one of them was about to turn up.

It was my father, and he wasn't alone. The pretty, petite woman with him looked a little shell-shocked.

"Oh my!" She gasped. "That's rather a strange experience, isn't it?"

My father took hold of her hand. "Are you okay, Blodwyn?"

"Yes, I think so. It's just that I've never attached myself to a human before. It's hard work, isn't it?"

"It gets easier." My father reassured her. "The first time I did it, I was exhausted too." He looked at me for the first time. "Jill, this is Blodwyn. I told you about her."

"Nice to meet you, Blodwyn."

"Nice to meet you too, Jill. I'm sorry, I'm a little disoriented. It's the first time I've done this."

"That's okay. I'm used to seeing ghosts on their first attachment."

Suddenly, the room became even colder, and my mother's ghost appeared. She was standing right next to Blodwyn.

"Oh? I'm so sorry, Jill. I had no idea that you had visitors." She turned to my father. "I'm surprised you remembered you had a daughter, Josh."

"Are you really going to drag that up again, Darlene? Jill knows the situation. I've already admitted to her that I wasn't a good father. I've apologised, and she's been gracious enough to accept my apology, and agree to make a new start."

"Jill is naïve. She doesn't know you like I do." My mother turned to Blodwyn, who had yet to say a word since my mother's arrival. "And you, lady. I hope you know what you're letting yourself in for."

"I—" Blodwyn began, but my father talked over her. "Don't try to poison Blodwyn with your hatred for me, Darlene."

"If this woman had any sense, she'd walk away now and keep on walking."

"Don't interfere in my life, Darlene. I don't try to tell you how to live your life—or death—whatever this is. I hear you've hooked up with some Welshman."

"Welsh-Italian, if you must know."

That was my cue to step in to try to defuse the situation.

"Blodwyn is Welsh-Italian too," I said.

"Italian-Welsh." Blodwyn corrected me.

My mother looked down her nose at Blodwyn.

"I think we should leave." My father took his new girlfriend's hand. "It's obvious that my ex-wife did this deliberately."

"Don't be ridiculous," my mother spat back. "Don't you think I have better things to do than waste my time with you and your new bit of skirt?"

"Hey!" My father reacted. "Do not refer to Blodwyn as a 'bit of skirt.' Come on Blodwyn, we're leaving."

And with that, the two of them disappeared.

"Mum! What was that all about?"

"What? I didn't even know they were here."

"Please don't treat me like an idiot. Of course you knew they were here. That's why you came."

"I was only trying to do the woman a favour—trying to warn her off. She'd thank me one day."

"Look, I know you and my father are never going to see eye to eye."

"That's the understatement of the year."

"But, I'm determined to at least give him the chance to make amends, and if he's now with Blodwyn, then I'm going to try to build a relationship with her too."

"Jill, you can't do—"

"Please." I put my hand up. "You have to respect my wishes."

"Just don't come running to me when everything goes wrong. Don't say I didn't warn you."

And with that, my mother disappeared too.

Sheesh! Who knew ghosts could be such hard work?

Chapter 24

When I left the office for the day, the last person I expected to bump into, was Mindy.

"Hi, Jill."

"Hello, Mindy," I said, coldly.

"Do you think I could have a quick word?"

"It will have to be quick. I'm in a hurry."

"Yeah, sure. I understand. Look, I know that Miles and I have caused you and your family a few problems."

"You think?"

"Okay, more than a few. But to be honest, I'm really tired of all this ill feeling between us. It's doing my head in. I just want to live a quiet life, and get on with our business without fighting all the time."

"You're talking to the wrong person. Don't you think perhaps you should be saying this to Miles? He was the one who had the idea to plant rats in Cuppy C. He was the one who opened a shop straight across the road from Grandma, tried to undercut her, and then used all sorts of underhand tactics to gain an unfair advantage. He even tried to open a P.I. business in Washbridge. I'm not sure why you're talking to me about stopping the aggravation."

"I know. You're right, but it's a bit more complicated than that."

"Complicated how? Just tell him to stop, or you'll leave him."

"I could never leave Miles."

"Well then, you'd better convince him to stop."

"I wish I could, but he's being influenced by other people."

"By who?"

"Can't you guess?"

"Not really."

"Come on, Jill. You must have seen them talking to him, giving him ideas."

"Do you mean Flora and Laura?"

"Who else? I can't believe the twins have been stupid enough to give those two girls somewhere to live and a job. They're bad news, Jill. They're seriously bad news."

I'd had my own suspicions about Flora and Laura for some time.

"What do you mean, Mindy? I'm going to need more than that. What exactly is it they're planning?"

"I don't know. They don't seem to trust me. They always try to catch Miles on his own, and then when I ask what they've been talking about, he's very cagey. It's almost as though they've told him not to share the information with me."

"Are you sure you're not just jealous of them?"

"No!" She looked outraged. "Miles and I are as close as we've ever been. But there's something dark about those two girls. Something evil. I just thought I should tell you. Maybe there's something you can do to get rid of them. Anyway, I have to go, otherwise Miles will wonder where I am."

What was I to make of that? I'd always had serious doubts about Flora and Laura, but I wasn't sure I could trust Mindy either. I wouldn't have put it past Miles to have orchestrated the whole thing. He could have persuaded Mindy to come to me with a sob story, just to get me to react and try to influence the twins. Before I said anything to them, I needed to find out more about the two ice maidens.

***

Thankfully, when I got home, there wasn't a train-stop blocking my way. I'd just got out of the car when I heard someone calling to me. It was Mrs Rollo. She was waving from her front door—beckoning me over. I just hoped she hadn't made any more cakes. It was getting more and more difficult to pretend to be appreciative of the monstrosities that she kept producing.

"Jill, I'm glad I caught you. There's been a man hanging around."

"What man? Hanging around where?"

"Around your house. I've seen him at least three times today. The first time I saw him, he was standing across the road, looking at your house. I thought it was a bit strange, but didn't worry too much about it. But then, a little later on, I was in the back garden seeing to my petunias, when I heard someone. I thought it was you or Jack, but when I looked over the fence, it was that same man. He was in your back garden. I asked who he was and what he was doing there. He said he knew you, and asked when you'd be back. I said it would be this evening. Then I saw him again, knocking at your door—it can't have been more than an hour ago. I came out, but as soon as I opened the door, he left."

"What did he look like?"

"He was very tall, with red hair and a red beard. Do you know him?"

"No, I don't think so. And you say he was here just over an hour ago?"

"Yes. I thought about calling the police the third time I saw him, but I didn't like to in case he really was a friend of yours. Anyway, I thought I should let you know."

"Thanks, Mrs Rollo." I turned to leave.

"Hold on a minute, Jill. I've made some muffins, and although I say it myself, they're rather delicious. I'll give you some for you and Jack."

"Oh, okay. Thanks."

She disappeared back into the house, and moments later, returned with a plateful of muffins. Allegedly.

"There are rather a lot there, Mrs Rollo."

"I know you young people have large appetites. And it's a shame to see them go to waste."

When I took the plate from her, it was so heavy that I almost dropped it. What on earth had she made the muffins with? Lead shot?

"Thanks very much, Mrs Rollo. I'm sure Jack will love these."

"My pleasure, dear. You can let me have the plate back any time. There's no hurry."

I put the plate of muffins on the breakfast bar, and then picked one of them up. It felt like a rock in my hand. I tried to break it in half, but it was solid.

I'd been home for no more than an hour when there was a knock at the door. Maybe it was the mysterious character who had been following me around—Damon or whatever his name was. If so, I was going to find out once and for all who he was, and what this was all about. But when I answered the door, it was Blake, and I could see that something was wrong.

"Can I come in, Jill?"

"Yes, of course." I led the way through to the living

room. "Are you okay, Blake?"

"No, not really."

"What's happened?"

"It's Jen."

"Is she all right?"

"She's fine. At least, she's not ill or anything."

"What's happened then?"

"It's my own stupid fault. I'd made myself a cup of green tea; Jen doesn't like it. I was carrying it upstairs when I tripped and spilled it on the landing. Have you ever spilled green tea, Jill?"

"I can't say I have."

"It leaves one heck of a stain. Jen was having a shower at the time, so I thought I'd be able to sort it out before she noticed. I hadn't realised that she'd heard me trip, and had opened the bathroom door to check what was going on. She saw."

"Saw what?"

"I knew I'd never get the stain out using normal cleaning materials, so I used the 'take it back' spell. The carpet was as good as new. I was feeling quite pleased with myself, but then I glanced up and saw Jen. She'd seen me use magic."

"What did you do?"

"What could I do? There was no way I could talk my way out of that. I had no choice. I had to use the 'forget' spell on her."

"I can understand why you're upset. I don't like using the 'forget' spell on Jack either, but sometimes it's unavoidable. It's just the price of living with a human."

"That's not it. I could live with that."

"What is it then?"

"The spell doesn't seem to have worked."

"What do you mean?"

"For a while, everything seemed to be okay. She was a little confused, like humans are after you've cast the 'forget' spell on them. But then later, she asked how I'd got rid of the stain. Somehow, she'd remembered that I'd spilled the tea. Fortunately, she hadn't remembered that I'd used magic to remove it. But she shouldn't have remembered any of it. It's like the 'forget' spell didn't work properly. I made some silly excuse and left. That's why I'm here now. I need your help."

"What can I do?"

"You're the most powerful witch. If *you* cast the 'forget' spell on Jen, it's bound to work."

"I wouldn't feel right about doing that."

"Please, Jill. I don't know what else to do."

"I'm not sure it's a good idea."

"Please—I'm desperate."

"Okay then."

Blake led the way across the road.

"Blake?" Jen came rushing to the door. "Where did you go?" Then she spotted me standing behind him. "Oh? Jill. I didn't know—"

I cast the 'forget' spell.

Jen looked a little dazed, but then smiled. "Come in, Jill. I'll make us all a drink."

While she was in the kitchen, I whispered to Blake, "You have to be more careful in future. I can't do this again."

"I know." He sighed. "It was bad enough when I knew I had the 'forget' spell to fall back on if something went wrong. What will I do now? I don't know if I can carry on like this."

"What alternative is there?"

"I could tell her the truth—that I'm a wizard."

"Are you being serious?"

"Yeah. Absolutely."

"Don't you realise what the consequences would be?"

"Yes, but you must have heard the stories. There are supposedly some couples, humans and sups, living together in Washbridge, where the sup has come clean with their partner. It can work if they both agree never to speak of it in public. That way the Rogue Retrievers never get to hear about it."

"I've heard the same stories, but do we actually know they're true? It's a very big risk to take. If you tell Jen, there's no un-telling her, and once she knows, there's no way of knowing how she'll react. She only has to tell one person—just one person—and if word gets back to Candlefield, the Rogue Retrievers will have no option but to take you back there. Do you really want to risk that?"

"I don't know what to do." He shook his head. "Carrying on like this seems impossible. Surely, being honest with Jen is better than this deceit. You must feel the same about Jack."

"Of course I do. I hate lying to Jack, but I've never seriously considered telling him. The risks are too high. You have to think this through, Blake. Don't do anything rash."

"Okay."

"Promise?"

"I promise."

It was hard seeing Blake upset like that. Not just

because I felt sorry for him, but because it made me even more aware of my own circumstances. It was like living on a knife edge all the time—always worried that something I might do or say would give the game away.

What would happen if Jack did find out I was a witch? Or if the 'forget' spell lost its effectiveness over a period of time when used on the same person? If I was taken back to Candlefield, it wasn't just Jack I'd lose. I'd never see Kathy, Peter and the kids again either. It made me wonder if having a human as a partner was really such a good idea. But it was too late to worry about that now. I thought the world of Jack, and couldn't imagine life without him. But could I really keep my secret from him indefinitely?

Jack didn't get home until eight o'clock because he'd been bowling with Megan. I hadn't been thrilled about the idea, but as he rightly pointed out, they needed to have at least one practice session together before the tournament. He'd asked if I wanted to go with them, but to be honest, I couldn't really bear the thought of watching those two together. At least this way I could pretend he was working late.

That was *until* he rolled in with a big smile on his face.

"How was the bowling?"

"Very good. Megan is really hot."

"Sorry?"

"At bowling, I mean. She beat me hands down."

"It's a good thing you're such a good loser, then."

"I didn't enjoy getting beaten, but if she's going to be my partner in the mixed doubles, then it's a good thing. She was really on fire. Everybody seemed to be watching her."

"What was she wearing?"

"Oh, the usual. Those shorts of hers and a vest top."

"No wonder everyone was watching her."

"Don't be catty, Jill. It doesn't suit you. What about you? How was your day?"

"Same old, same old. Mrs Rollo gave us some muffins. They're on the breakfast bar."

"What are they like?"

"I don't know. I haven't dared try one. And to be honest, unless you're fully paid up with your dental insurance, I wouldn't recommend you do either. They're like rocks. Have you had anything to eat?"

"Yeah, we grabbed a hot dog at the bowling alley. I wouldn't mind a cup of tea, though."

"You know where the kettle is. And while you're at it, you can make one for me."

We sat at the breakfast bar to drink our tea. I was munching my way through a small plateful of custard creams. They helped to take away the images of Megan and Jack bowling together.

"I heard some shocking news today," Jack said, more serious now. "You must keep this under your hat because it hasn't yet been released to the press."

"You know me. I'm the soul of discretion."

He rolled his eyes, but carried on anyway. "There may be another serial killer in Washbridge."

"What do you mean *another*? There has never been one to the best of my knowledge. If you remember, 'The Animal' turned out not to be a serial killer at all."

"We don't need to go back over that old ground again."

Jack didn't like to be reminded of The Animal murder case. It was not long after he'd moved to Washbridge. The press and the police had thought they were looking for a serial killer, but in fact it had turned out to be two different murderers, both of whom I'd helped to bring to justice.

"Anyway, you were saying?" I prompted him.

"Apparently, there have been two victims so far."

"Two? Isn't that a bit early to class it as a serial killing?"

"Normally yes, but it's the circumstances. From what I understand, both victims have near-identical puncture marks on their necks. The guys back at Washbridge station are dubbing him The Vampire."

Oh, bum!

Chapter 25

The next morning, as I was walking from the car to the office, I spotted the headline on The Bugle. It read: *'The Vampire.'*

I popped into the newsagent to buy a copy. The lead article was typically sensationalist. It covered the two murders that Jack had mentioned the previous night. Somehow, The Bugle had got hold of the story, and got wind of the puncture marks found on the necks of the victims. Needless to say, The Bugle had made a big thing of this, and suggested there was a vampire in our midst.

The last thing I needed was The Bugle instilling fear into the residents of Washbridge. It came as no surprise to find the article was attributed to my old friend, Dougal Bugle. A smaller article, at the bottom of the front page, reported that Arthur Longstaff, CEO of Tip Top Construction, had been charged with the murder of Joseph Lewis. Result!

I made a quick phone call.

"Daze, I don't know if you've seen it, but The Bugle's headline is 'The Vampire'."

"Yeah, I've seen it. I'd been hoping we could keep this thing under wraps."

"According to Jack, two bodies have been found already, both with puncture marks on their necks."

"There'll be more. You can bet your life on that. We're rounding up the rogue vampires as quickly as we can. We've already shipped five of them back to Candlefield, but it's likely there'll be more. Bar Scarlet had a huge clientele. If only a small percentage of those turn rogue, we'll have major problems. This publicity can only make things worse."

"Please, keep me posted, Daze."

When I arrived at the office, Jules was behind the desk, and for once she wasn't knitting.

"Morning, Jill." She beamed.

"Morning, Jules. You're looking particularly pleased with life. Could it have anything to do with a certain young man named Jethro?"

"We had our first date last night. He took me to Bar Piranha. Do you know it?"

"Yes, I've been there a few times."

"It's great, isn't it? There are all these tanks with piranhas in them. I was a bit scared at first, but Jethro said he wouldn't let the piranhas get me." She giggled.

"I take it you had a good evening?"

"It was brilliant. He's such an interesting guy. He's had all kinds of jobs, you know. Some of them in places I've never even heard of. He was even in a dance troupe once, and he's done some modelling. But then—" She blushed. "He does have the body for it. At the end of the evening, he insisted on walking me to my door. He said it wasn't safe to be out by myself because of this vampire serial killer. Have you heard about the murders, Jill? The victims have vampire bites on their necks."

"I wouldn't believe everything you read. The Bugle always blows things out of all proportion. There are no such things as vampires."

"I'm not so sure. Perhaps there are. And werewolves and witches too. We just don't know."

"It's all nonsense. I wouldn't give it another thought."

I started towards my office door, but Jules called me

back.

"Jill, I'm booking the Wool Con tickets today, for me and Mrs V."

"Okay. Let me know when it is, so I know you'll both be off that day."

"We'd really like you to come with us."

"Wool isn't really my thing."

"Please, Jill. It'll be like a company day out. You know, team building, that sort of thing. Mrs V wants you to come, and I do too. Please say you will."

"Okay. I suppose so, but I'm not getting dressed up as a ball of wool."

***

It was a slow day with nothing much happening. Even Winky was keeping himself to himself. I think he'd tired himself out building the time machine. He was fast asleep under the sofa when Zac, my landlord, popped in. Zac cut a much more impressive figure since he'd got rid of that stupid toupee. He now thoroughly embraced his baldness. Maybe I should mention it to Toby Jugg. He was another one who definitely should have given up the toupee.

"Hi, Zac, how's things?"

"Hello, Jill. I won't take up much of your time. I just wanted to check that you found the book I left for you."

"What book?"

"I popped in with it the other day while you were out. Your young lady said to drop it on your desk."

"What kind of book was it?"

"A children's book."

I reached into my top drawer, and brought out 'squeaky

book.'

"Was it this one?"

"Yes, that's the one. One of the workmen found it in a cupboard when they were knocking the rooms together next door. I said I'd let you have it. It's got your name in the back."

"And you say you left it on my desk?"

"Yes, and I left a scribbled note to explain where it was found."

"Okay, Zac. Thanks very much. I had this book when I was a child. I guess my father must have put it in the cupboard."

"No problem."

I glanced over at the sofa. Winky was awake now, and looking rather sheepish.

"Get over here!"

***

A clear-out of my old case files was long overdue. Jack wasn't going to be in until late, so I decided to make a start on them. Winky was hiding under the sofa, still smarting from the tongue-lashing I'd given him earlier. After Zac's visit, it hadn't taken me long to work out what had happened.

Winky must have seen the book and the note on my desk. He'd read the note and from there, plotted his little scam. My father had hated squeaky book. It used to drive him crazy. He must have hidden it away in one of the cupboards next door. I'd always assumed it had been lost. The book had stayed there until the workmen found it. They gave it to Zac, who put it on my desk.

That's when Winky had decided he'd try to get one over on me. All that stuff about time travel had been complete nonsense. He'd only done it so he could get me to have a bet with him. The so-called time machine was nothing more than a metal cabinet. He'd used the steam as a screen to sneak away and hide. When he came back, he'd produced squeaky book, and given me some cock-and-bull story about how mini-me had given the book to him. And sucker here, had fallen for it hook, line, and sinker. I'd even paid him out on his bet.

After discovering the truth, I'd given him an ultimatum: pay me back the money by next week, and dismantle the so-called time machine, or find somewhere else to live. He hadn't put up a fight—I was pretty sure he didn't care about the money. It was all about getting one over on me.

It was a pity that the time machine didn't work. It would have been nice to go back in time to see my adoptive parents again—to have one last chance to talk to them both. I still lived in hope that one day they'd appear to me as ghosts, just as my birth family had, but so far there was no sign of that happening.

I decided to call it a day.

"I'm going home now, Winky. Don't forget to dismantle the time machine, and to repay my money."

"Don't worry. I'm on it."

It was very quiet; Jules had long since gone home. As I stepped out of the office, onto the landing, I noticed a trail of what appeared to be blood on the floor. I followed it to a small cupboard further down the corridor. The door wasn't locked. Inside the cupboard, lying on the floor was the man who'd been stalking me for several days. The man with red hair, and a red beard. The man who had said his name was Damon.

I checked his pulse, but he was dead. There was a large wound in his chest. It appeared he'd been stabbed, but there was no sign of a knife. I made a call to Leo Riley, and fifteen minutes later, he and two uniformed officers came charging up the stairs.

I was at Washbridge police station for three hours, where I was asked all kinds of ridiculous questions by Riley. I'd told him how I'd found the body, and said that was all I knew, but he kept pressing me for more information. I didn't tell him that the man had been to my office and my house. If I had, I would never have got out of there.

I'd phoned Jack from the police station, but only after it had taken me an hour to persuade Riley to allow me to make the call. Jack had wanted to come in, but I'd told him to stay at home. I knew if he came, he'd end up going head-to-head with Riley.

"What happened?" Jack asked when I finally made it home.

"Nothing much. I've just had to put up with three hours of Riley and his moronic questions. I told him everything I know. Which is nothing."

"Are you sure?"

"Of course I'm sure."

I probably should have told Jack that the man had been stalking me, but I wanted to find out who he was first.

"Could he have been another victim of The Vampire?" Jack asked.

"Don't tell me you've started calling the murderer 'The

Vampire'?"

"It seems appropriate now. There's been a third murder, you know."

"You mean in addition to the man I found?"

"Yeah, and this one had the same puncture mark to the neck."

"My guy didn't, but he did have a big puncture wound to his chest. He'd been stabbed."

"What about the murder weapon?"

"There was no sign of it."

Eventually Jack stopped with the third degree, and we settled down to a glass of wine. I needed one after the day I'd had.

Jack glanced at the mantelpiece. "Do you think there's any chance that Kathy will ever bring back the snow globe?"

"Look Jack, I'm sorry, but I didn't tell you the truth about that."

"What do you mean?"

"I didn't give it to Kathy. I dropped it on the kitchen floor, and it smashed."

"Why didn't you tell me?"

"I should have done. I just felt bad about it because it was such a lovely gift. I'm so clumsy. I thought I might be able to find an identical one, but I couldn't."

"I don't care about the snow globe, but I do care that you didn't tell me. I thought you'd agreed that you weren't going to keep secrets. You said there'd be no more lies."

"I know, and there won't be. Not from now on, I promise."

"Are you sure there's nothing else I should know

about?"
"Positive. I have no more secrets."

ALSO BY ADELE ABBOTT

The Witch P.I. Mysteries:

Witch Is When... (Books #1 to #12)
Witch Is When It All Began
Witch Is When Life Got Complicated
Witch Is When Everything Went Crazy
Witch Is When Things Fell Apart
Witch Is When The Bubble Burst
Witch Is When The Penny Dropped
Witch Is When The Floodgates Opened
Witch Is When The Hammer Fell
Witch Is When My Heart Broke
Witch Is When I Said Goodbye
Witch Is When Stuff Got Serious
Witch Is When All Was Revealed

Witch Is Why... (Books #13 to #24)
Witch Is Why Time Stood Still
Witch is Why The Laughter Stopped
Witch is Why Another Door Opened
Witch is Why Two Became One
Witch is Why The Moon Disappeared
Witch is Why The Wolf Howled
Witch is Why The Music Stopped
Witch is Why A Pin Dropped
Witch is Why The Owl Returned
Witch is Why The Search Began
Witch is Why Promises Were Broken
Witch is Why It Was Over

The Susan Hall Mysteries:
Whoops! Our New Flatmate Is A Human.
Whoops! All The Money Went Missing.
Whoops! There's A Canary In My Coffee
See web site for availability.

AUTHOR'S WEB SITE
http:www.AdeleAbbott.com

FACEBOOK
http://www.facebook.com/AdeleAbbottAuthor

MAILING LIST
(new release notifications only)
http:/AdeleAbbott.com/adele/new-releases/

Printed in Great Britain
by Amazon